A Heart Divided

Anjuli Rajprasad is a U.S. based attorney. She earned her *Juris Doctor* from the University of Maryland Francis King Carey School of Law. A Company Secretary by qualification and training, Anjuli worked with the Securities and Exchange Board of India, Mumbai, in the Enforcement, Surveillance, and Investigation departments. After moving to the USA, she worked with the finance teams at the Johns Hopkins University and the Johns Hopkins Health System before gaining experience with public interest law groups. Her writing journey began a decade ago with contributions to the *Chicken Soup for the Indian Soul* series. She has also written several blog posts on issues dealing with social stigma, and regularly posts her views on Twitter and Instagram under the handle @incognito_river. *A Heart Divided* is her debut novel.

A Heart Divided

Anjuli Rajprasad

Om Books International

First published in 2023 by

Om Books International

Corporate & Editorial Office
A-12, Sector 64, Noida 201 301
Uttar Pradesh, India
Phone: +91 120 477 4100
Email: editorial@ombooks.com
Website: www.ombooksinternational.com

Sales Office
107, Ansari Road, Darya Ganj,
New Delhi 110 002, India
Phone: +91 11 4000 9000
Email: sales@ombooks.com
Website: www.ombooks.com

ISBN: 978-93-92834-08-0

Printed in India

10 9 8 7 6 5 4 3 2 1

For my husband, Raj

Contents

1

Mumbai

The sound of the waves, even amid the silence of midnight, wasn't loud enough to mask the thoughts screaming inside Neeti's head as she sat on the concrete platform at Bandstand, mindlessly watching the waves hit the rocks. It was therapeutic.

This wasn't the first time Neeti was here. It was her treasured spot, where she had spent numerous evenings with the very person she was now trying to get over. Now this place only brought back painful memories; the promises to remain together for the "rest of our lives" were just promises, after all. Mere words—shallow, meaningless words.

She closed her eyes and took off the hair tie to let her curly tresses flow with the wind, soaking in the sound of the waves as some drops of water hit her face. Lost in thought, she didn't attempt to wipe them off. All she could think of was Ruchir's hazel eyes. Ruchir wasn't the first guy who had come into Neeti's life, but she had hoped that he would be the last. She wanted him to be the last. He was all she desired. Neeti was in her fool's paradise assuming that Ruchir also wanted her, but her belief was far removed from reality. That's the thing with relationships—you spend countless nights absorbed in your dulcet dreams, only to wake up to harsh reality.

Getting over someone is never an event; it's a process, and you can't decide how long it would take. It happens on its own, and it decides its duration. You just witness it all as a third person. You struggle to get over someone for days, sometimes years, and then one fine day you wake up realizing that you are over them. The songs don't remind you of them, the places you hung out with them don't scare you anymore, and the memories aren't painful any longer. In fact, there are no memories at all, and then you wonder why in the world were you suffering for so long! But that realization comes only with time. Slow and steady wins the race, but at what cost—nobody tells us that. You lose sleep, peace, and appetite, all for someone who couldn't care less.

You don't reach the decision to get over a person in an instant. You want to live in denial for as long as you possibly can. Then finally one day, you give in, and once you decide that it's time, you ask yourself, 'Come on, I have decided to move on, why am I still stuck!?' You get questions in your head you have no answers to, the questions you thought would magically disappear because you have now decided to move on! Much to your dismay, those questions are still there, just like the millions of stars you don't see during the day but they make a quiet appearance when it's all dark. And that's when you end up alone at Bandstand, watching the waves make love to the rocks.

Neeti took an auto-rickshaw to return home. The welled-up tears finally found their way down her cheeks as she started climbing the stairs to reach her apartment.

'It's over,' Neeti told Rhea over the phone.

'It was over a long time back, Neeti. Wait, I am coming to your place,' Rhea said. She could hear Neeti sobbing.

'No, it's too late right now. Just talk to me.'

'I will talk to you the whole night if you want me to. Now tell me what happened?'

'You know, Rhea, when people die, we live with the memories of the relationship we had had with them, but when a relationship dies, you are left with nothing.'

'Not everything is meant to be in our life, and maybe something better is written for you.'

'I did not want better.'

'What did Ruchir say?'

'He is getting married.'

'To?'

'That doesn't matter, does it?'

'Get a hold of yourself, Neeti. You are stronger than you think.'

'I am weak.'

'Only the strong can accept that they are weak.'

'I was blaming myself for this breakup all this while, I thought it was my insecurities. I did not know people move out of love so easily. What an elusive concept love is! You think you are in love with someone, assuming that they are also in love with you, only to realize that it was all a sham.'

'Love is not to be blamed. Humans are flawed. We fail love, love never fails us. You can't stay alone right now, please let me know if you want me to come and stay with you for some time.'

'Why can't people be forthright and let the other person know that they aren't in love anymore? I was completely blindsided.'

'Some people fear that it might hurt the other person.'

'As if this isn't hurting.'

'I really don't know what to say. What he did was probably not the best thing to do, but what you are doing to yourself is even worse. Let me come to your place.'

'Don't worry, I will be fine.'

'You don't sound fine to me.'

'It will take time.'

'Let me come.'

'I will be fine. I am feeling better after talking to you. It's too late now, also, we have office tomorrow. You sleep, I will try to sleep as well.'

'Okay Neeti, take care. Wake me up if you need to talk again. I will see you in the office tomorrow.'

Neeti went to the office the next day, but was feeling listless and decided to leave office early. Thankfully, it was a Friday and she had two days to put herself back together.

'*Didi*, how much will you cry! Stop now,' Vandana said.

Vandana was Neeti's domestic help who was more like a sister. Although older than Neeti, she called her '*didi*'. Vandana took care of the household chores for Neeti and on weekends they also had chat sessions in the morning. On Saturday and Sunday mornings, Vandana would make ginger tea for both of them and they would sit on the bean bags and chit-chat. No, not the kind of gossip you might be imagining. There were no conversations about who was sleeping with whom in the apartment complex; they discussed things in general, about their lives, and the world around them.

But today, Neeti was in bed. She did not want to get up.

'Get up now, *didi*, it's almost noon. We need to forget the ones who don't remember us. Please get up, I have made awesome ginger tea, come, let's have it, else it would get cold,'

Vandana said, adjusting the pleats of her yellow floral printed saree, getting ready to relax and have tea with Neeti after finishing all the chores.

'You have your tea, Vandana. I don't feel like having anything,' Neeti said, pulling the sheet over her face. She turned around and buried her face in her pillow.

'You will fall sick like this, *didi*. You are so far away from your parents. How would they feel if they get to know that you have fallen sick?'

'Don't blackmail me, Vandana. As it is life is playing dirty games with me.'

'Get up *na*, *didi*, please.'

Neeti finally got up. Vandana drew open the curtains and the room brightened up, so did Neeti's face after having tea with Vandana. It brought a smile on Neeti's face. We don't always realize how addictive sadness is and how difficult it is to get out of the clutches of sadness alone. Neeti was thankful that she had Vandana with her this morning. If not for Vandana's coaxing she would have remained in bed all day.

'How is your daughter doing?' Neeti asked Vandana.

'She is learning to work on computers these days. *Didi*, I don't want her to work as domestic help, I want her to work the way you do ... in some big office.'

'What you do is nothing to be ashamed of.'

'I know that but tell me how many people respect our work? No one wants to do household work, and no one thinks highly of those who do it, people only admire the ones who are educated and work in big offices.'

'That's true, I am not sure who made these rules, but that's how our world has become. Let me tell you something, however—never feel ashamed of what you do, you are helping people like me and we could not be more grateful to you and others like you. Without you and people like you who do household work for us, our lives would be a mess. Having said that, I really hope your daughter gets the best of education, because in today's time that's necessary, not just to succeed in life, but also to get a better perspective. I am sure your daughter will do well in life; she has got the best mom.'

There was a knock at the door. Vandana opened it. It was Rhea.

'How are you, *didi*?' Vandana asked Rhea.

'I'm well. How are you doing?' Rhea chipped in.

'I'm fine, please come in.'

'Where is our female *Devdas*?'

'*Arey didi, kya aap bhi*. She is fine now, we just had tea together.'

Rhea was Neeti's colleague and best friend, and Neeti trusted her more than she trusted herself. Rhea was the first and only friend Neeti had made in Mumbai. She had never imagined that in a city where there was no dearth of people, finding a friend would be such a challenge. But she was happy to have found Rhea, who was in fact Neeti's strength and support system in Mumbai.

Rhea was tall and dusky. Her skin shone like porcelain. Perhaps, it was her kindness that reflected on her face. She had big, round eyes, which gave away the fact that she was Bengali. She had long, dark hair which she always tied in a neat ponytail, and her bangs covered her bright shiny forehead. She spoke almost perfect Hindi, and no points for guessing that her Bangla was impeccable too. She spoke Bangla over the phone whenever she talked to her family, and the only phrase Neeti understood was *Theek ache* which meant 'Okay'. Rhea had cherubic innocence and the boldness of a warrior princess. But above all these attributes, it was her sense of humour that won hearts and made people around her absolutely comfortable with her.

'How are you feeling now?' Rhea asked.

'Better. Vandana was a great help. I was drowning, her ginger tea saved me,' Neeti said with a smile.

'Thanks to Vandana, at least your apartment isn't a mess like you. Now, go and change into something quickly. Let's go and have your favourite sandwich.'

'*Didi*, shall I make tea for you?' Vandana asked Rhea.

'No, we are going out now. I will have it some other time,' Rhea replied.

Every day, before going to office, Neeti and Rhea would stop by the street vendors to have breakfast. Most days they would have veggie cheese sandwiches which were popularly known as Mumbai-style sandwiches. It was a Saturday, as Neeti loved those sandwiches and Rhea wanted to make Neeti feel better, Rhea insisted that they go and have one even though they didn't have to go to work.

'I'm sure you will feel a lot better after having the sandwich,' Rhea continued.

Neeti had a favourite street vendor because he used her preferred brand of butter and cheese. The best part besides, of course, eating those delectable sandwiches was to watch the vendor make them, which almost felt like watching someone create an enchanting symphony. He would prepare the bread slices first, by cutting off the edges and smearing butter on both the slices. He would then apply green *chutney* on both the slices, and would then take the veggies in his palms and spread them over the bread slices, cucumber first, followed by boiled potatoes, green bell peppers, and finally, onions. Then came the cheese which the vendor grated over the veggies, much to Neeti's heart's content. He would then heat up the sandwich toaster on a gas stove, dabbing butter on both the sides of the toaster. A sizzling sound indicated that the toaster was ready. He would place the sandwich inside the toaster, onto the stove, toasting each side, one by one. Carefully taking the sandwich out of the toaster, he would meticulously cut the sandwich into bite-size pieces and would serve it with tomato ketchup on the side. Not entirely sure what secret ingredient he used to put in the sandwiches that they tasted so heavenly.

Neeti gazed at the whole process every day but still got excited every morning to watch it again as if she were watching it for the first time.

They reached Nariman Point and Neeti was pleasantly surprised to see her favourite vendor there, despite being a Saturday and post lunchtime. They grabbed their sandwiches and sat on the curbside.

'Why do we always choose the wrong ones,' Neeti asked Rhea.

'To recognize the right ones when we find them.'

'The worst part is that when someone wrongs you, they try to make you feel that you were wrong all along.'

'I know, and it sucks, but no one wants to accept that they are depraved, it's not easy.'

'I wish I had never met Ruchir. At times I wonder why did it happen.'

'You will get over him, just give it some time. People fall out of love, some are never in love, to begin with, you can never tell for sure. He has moved on; he is getting married. You need to stop thinking about him,' Rhea said as she put the last bite of sandwich in her mouth.

'You can't turn it off just like that, it's not a switch.'

'I get that, but you need to be strong and let go. Finish your sandwich now.'

'Shall I try to call him one last time?'

'To get an invite to his wedding? Or do you think you are a Hindi film hero that would make a phone call on the wedding day and the bride would come running to you? Come out of your cloud cuckoo land and just let go.'

'It feels bad that things had to end this way.'

'There's never a good way to end relationships. Just give it a little time and focus on yourself.'

'Do you realize how thankful I am that I have you?'

'Don't jinx it, let's go home.'

Neeti was alone but Rhea made sure she wasn't lonely. Rhea was with Neeti on most weekends and they would have sleepovers at times.

'I think the main lead of the movie should retire,' Rhea said after they finished watching a movie.

'This was his debut film!' Neeti said and they burst out laughing.

'I liked Ruchir a lot.'

'I know; we tend to like things that aren't good for us.'

'Ugh, let's go to bed, you are mean!'

It was Rhea's ability to make others laugh that helped Neeti through her breakup. As people often say 'laughter is the best medicine', and when you have someone to share your laughs with, it's a cherry on top.

One morning after breakfast, Rhea looked at Neeti and said that she wanted to talk to her. Rhea wasn't sure how Neeti would react to it but she was certain that after having her favourite sandwich, Neeti would be in a good mood, so perhaps that was the best time for her to break the news to Neeti.

'Guess what!' Rhea was ecstatic. Neeti saw an elated Rhea and discerned that she must have received approval for her transfer to Kolkata, which she had been earnestly trying for the last six months.

'You are leaving me.'

'I never can.'

They hugged. Neeti congratulated Rhea and was happy for her, but deep down she knew it would not be easy for her to function without Rhea.

'Promise me you will be fine,' Rhea said, with a tear silently escaping the corner of her eye.

'I don't make promises that I can't keep, but I promise I will try. I will try my best,' Neeti said with a smile. Her eyes were shining brightly with the tears she was trying to hide, albeit unsuccessfully.

'Every time you miss me, come here and have two sandwiches, one for yourself and one for me. In a few days, you would gain an enormous amount of weight and then you would spend all your time in the gym to lose all those kilos and will forget about me.'

'Oh, God! I will miss this so much!'

Neeti helped Rhea pack her bags and soon it was time to leave. On the way to the railway station, they stopped at Nariman Point and had their favourite Mumbai-style sandwich together for the last time. They took a cab from Nariman Point to Chhatrapati Shivaji Maharaj Terminus (CST) and looked for Rhea's coach. Rhea lifted one handle of the bag and Neeti held on to the other side, and they were able to move the heaviest of the bags together. Neeti carried another piece of luggage that had wheels so it was convenient to move it, and Rhea carried a backpack and another bag on her shoulder. They placed all the luggage under the berth and sat inside the coach for some time.

The coach smelled of Indian food and happiness. Everyone in the coach seemed joyful except for Neeti; her eyes were wet and heart heavy.

'I am going to miss you too, Neeti. Please take care of yourself. I will remain worried about you,' said Rhea as she teared up a little and her voice started cracking. She then glanced at her watch and realized that it was almost 10 p.m. and Neeti would have to go home alone from there. 'Go now, it's too late. You don't have to stay at the station until the train departs,' Rhea said with concern.

'I will be fine, I am not leaving until the train leaves,' said Neeti as a tear finally rolled down her cheek.

The train signalled to start with a whistle and Neeti hugged Rhea one last time as she uttered, 'I am going to miss you, Rhea, but I am happy for you. You are going back to your people.' It was time to bid each other goodbye, to wish the best for Rhea's new chapter in life, and to treasure all the memories that they had made together. Neeti got off the train and the train started moving slowly. As she waved to Rhea, Neeti watched the train gain momentum. Rhea waved back screaming, 'Go home!' Neeti stood there on the railway platform, numb, until she could no longer see Rhea. In a matter of a few seconds, the train was out of sight.

Rhea got married to Pranab, her long-time boyfriend, six months after they moved to Kolkata. Rhea wanted a transfer to Kolkata because Pranab had been offered a well-paying job there, but he did not want to move away from Rhea, so he continued with his first job in Mumbai. He had been working in the same capacity for three years and was not offered a promotion despite being tremendously competent. He was desperate to move to Kolkata but Rhea was in Mumbai and he didn't want to move there alone. Their families also lived in

Kolkata so it made even more sense for Rhea to move to the same city. Neeti and Rhea would speak over the phone after she moved, with time the phone calls gradually decreased as Rhea got busy with her married life.

With Rhea gone, Neeti was left alone in Mumbai, and she decided to shift her focus back to where she belonged. She began spending weekends in the office now as it was time to move on with life. Easier said than done, but Neeti had decided to give it a try. As Rhea said, not all relationships are meant to be, and one needs to understand before it gets too late. Neeti did move on, but not to anyone else. She wanted to give herself time—to heal, to recover, and to feel ready to take on life as it comes. Fortunately, she was assigned a pivotal role in a high-profile investigation involving a dematerialization scam. The work was challenging and involved working late hours and weekends as well, just the way she liked it. Although Neeti was a part of the surveillance team, Shekhar, who was heading the investigations team on this case, had made a special request to Neeti's department to let her work on this investigation. He had been observing Neeti for a while and was impressed by her sincerity towards her work, and work ethic. Shekhar and Neeti would spend long hours trying to figure out how a bunch of people managed to dupe companies and in turn innocent investors. Neeti was personally invested in the case because that would mean bringing justice to people who had been deprived of getting any shares in the initial public offerings of several companies over a period of time.

'I wonder what people get by deceiving others,' Neeti said.

'Quick money,' Shekhar responded.

'I don't think money will ever become so important for me that I will be okay with cheating others.'

'These are nefarious people and don't think like you and me, Neeti. They have a different mindset. Money is a solution to a lot of problems in the world, and the root cause of many problems at the same time.'

'Makes sense. But don't they have a fear of getting caught?'

'Now we have you as an investigator, they must fear to do such things from now on.'

'Come on, Shekhar. You need to stop treating me like a kid.'

'I don't, I was just trying to pull your leg.'

'All right, let's get back to work.'

Neeti's days were now getting spent sifting through huge piles of investigation files, examining and trying to understand the money trail, and analysing data. It was not an easy case to crack and even though both Neeti and Shekhar had established prima facie that there was a scam, they needed solid evidence to nab the perpetrators.

It was 9.30 p.m. and Neeti was still in the office. She decided to call it a night and wrap up. The city was wide awake with cabs lining up outside her office. She grabbed a sandwich before taking a cab to CST. She was about to board the 10 p.m. local when her cellphone rang.

'Neeti, guess what! We finally have the evidence! Do you remember what you had suggested? Come over to the office and I will explain it to you,' Shekhar said. He was still in the office, working on the case.

Neeti was thrilled to hear this and rushed back. Luckily, Mumbai never sleeps and the cab drivers are no different, she took a cab from CST and reached the office in fifteen minutes. 'You are still here? Now you are making me feel guilty about leaving early, but tell me what you found. I can't wait!'

'It's 10 p.m., Neeti, you need to go a little easy on yourself. I know you were here until 9.30 p.m. I saw you leaving the office but I didn't want to hold you up at that time because I was not sure if I had concrete evidence, but as soon as you left, I thought of what you had suggested and it actually is the case.'

'So, you mean the perpetrators did indeed take photographs and names from matrimonial profiles and then created fake demat accounts using those photos and names, to get as many shares as possible in the IPOs of the companies we are looking into?'

'Absolutely!'

'They were getting way more shares than they could legally get as retail investors, all by creating these fake demat accounts.'

'Yes, and now we have all the evidence to prove that they got all these shares that did not belong to them, they made huge profits by getting these shares at lower prices in the IPOs, and selling them in the market once the prices shot up, depriving many genuine investors of getting any shares at all.'

Neeti gave Shekhar a high five. 'We've finally cracked the case!'

'This is huge, you have no idea what this means, this will create news.'

'Everything we do creates news anyway.'

'You don't realize what you have done.'

'What *we* have done.'

It had taken a massive number of man-hours to finally solve the case. After six months of gruelling investigation, Neeti, Shekhar, and others in the team were able to solve the case and catch hold of the perpetrators. Neeti was delighted—for herself, for the team that had worked day in and out on this investigation, and most importantly, for the investors.

'Thanks, Shekhar. I can't put into words how happy I feel being a part of the investigation,' Neeti told Shekhar the next day.

'Do you realize how thankful I am to you? I came to you every time I was stuck. You don't realize what an asset you are,' Shekhar responded.

Neeti smiled as she walked towards her desk. Other projects were waiting for her attention as she was spending all her time on this single investigation for the last six months.

Neeti finished her work for the day and went to Marine Drive later that evening for a stroll at the promenade and then sat there reminiscing about how she had moved to Mumbai with dreams of a successful professional life. The first six months of the stay in Mumbai were the most difficult. In the beginning, she got startled by the sheer volume of human beings the city held. But once she got over the peripheral unsettling chaos, she saw the triumph of the human spirit defying all odds and admired the way life bloomed in seemingly hopeless places and corners of the city. Marine Drive was accurately the heart of the city, adorned by the 'Queen's necklace'. The hustle and bustle of Mumbai makes life seem like a clockwork machine. But here at Marine Drive, with the cool breeze blowing, time came to a standstill. Neeti took the breeze in and closed her eyes. What a blessing it was to be alive! She was thankful for everything that happened in the office recently and was missing Rhea and also her parents.

She called her parents and gave them the news. They were overjoyed that their little girl was doing them proud. She also called Rhea and she congratulated Neeti and wished she were with Neeti on her special day. Neeti went back and could not sleep; she was exhilarated. She spent the Saturday at home letting the success at work sink in. On Sunday morning when she was fast asleep, her cellphone rang. She picked it up, not entirely pleased about her sleep being disturbed.

'Neeti, did you read today's newspaper?' the voice on the other side exclaimed.

'Come on, it's a Sunday. I am sleeping. Who is it?' Neeti replied in a flustered tone. She was annoyed. She hardly got to sleep properly on weekdays and was not too pleased that her sleep was getting disturbed on a Sunday too.

'This is Vivek, Vivek Anand. Go grab today's newspaper, you are a star.'

'Last I knew, I was a human. When did I transform into a star? Vivek, please let me sleep. I will talk to you later.'

'Neeti! Your name is in the newspaper! There's a whole article on the investigation you completed recently,' said Vivek. He sounded excited and happy for Neeti.

'Stop kidding me. Is it April fool's day today?'

'Wake up, Neeti! Do you want me to come to your apartment and show the news article to you?'

'No, it's okay. I will have a look at it. I still don't believe you though, but now that you have woken me up, let me run to Ramya's place and see if she gets this particular newspaper.'

Vivek was Neeti's colleague. They were hired in the same batch and lived in the apartments provided by the company in the same apartment complex. Neeti got up and walked up to Ramya's apartment, which was right next door. She asked Ramya if she had a copy of the newspaper Vivek just told Neeti about. It was a leading national daily. Neeti had subscribed to another newspaper, and today she was almost regretting it. She was excited to read the news story but was not entirely happy about disturbing someone else this early on a Sunday morning.

'*...It was days of hard work of the team comprising M. Shekhar and his teammate Neeti Singh that such a huge scam was identified and the perpetrators were caught...*' the article read. Neeti thanked Ramya and gave the newspaper back. Ramya looked at Neeti with a straight face. She wasn't at all amused by the fact that Neeti's name was in the paper.

'Well, I will see you later,' Neeti said as she rushed to the market to get a copy of her own. A five-rupee newspaper never felt so valuable to her. She kept staring at it for at least ten minutes and then cut the article and added it to the file she had been keeping that contained her credentials. The next morning, everyone at work treated her like a star.

'You did it!'

'We are so proud of you.'

'This is a huge accomplishment.'

The compliments kept pouring in. 'Shekhar, was it you? Did you give my name to be published in the newspaper?' Neeti asked.

'You deserved it, Neeti. I haven't done any favours to you. You got the recognition that was rightfully yours,' Shekhar said.

Neeti was surrounded by people almost the entire day. It was the best day of her life. She kept receiving compliments the whole day and it was a little too much for her liking. She was overwhelmed and left for home earlier than usual that day.

She got a promotion and a two-bedroom apartment from the company. She was alone and an apartment that big started to make her feel lonely. First it was Ruchir and then Rhea had to leave too. Neeti started blogging every night after coming home from work to fill the void in her life. In a few months' time, she was able to make a couple of online friends with whom she began chatting regularly. She got in touch with an NGO through those friends and decided to spend her weekends volunteering for it.

2

Mihir

Shishir Vatsa was the founder of an NGO, Prayaas, which focused on getting people involved in creating a better future for society, starting with mentoring young adults. His idea behind creating this NGO was that the very step towards doing something great is trying, hence the name Prayaas. Neeti had come to Prithvi Café to attend their weekly meeting. She had been attending these meetings for about six months now and was thankful to have found something constructive to do to fill the void in her life. For some reason, all other members and volunteers, besides Shishir, had decided to not show up that day. Mihir, a friend of Shishir's, had randomly decided to drop by, only to be disappointed seeing no one turn up. He believed that *chai* could cure everything, so he decided to fix his disappointment with a cup of *Irani chai*. By the time he went to order it, Neeti had finally reached Prithvi Café. She was walking towards Shishir and as she crossed the crowded cash counter, she heard a strong and firm voice which made her head turn.

'*Dada, do Irani chai aur do bun-maska*, please,' said a guy wearing a crisp white shirt, blue denims, and black sandals.

Neeti went and joined Shishir at the table, as she saw the guy in white walk towards their table. He walked in a seemingly careless fashion as his broad shoulders created an indelible impression on Neeti's mind. She could write a poem about those shoulders, she thought. She was convinced that he didn't even notice her and was flummoxed as to why he was walking towards her, completely forgetting that another human being was sitting on the other side of the table.

'Neeti, this is my friend Mihir Varma. Mihir, this is one of our volunteers, Neeti Singh,' Shishir said, introducing Mihir and Neeti to each other.

'Hi, Neeti,' Mihir said, with a smile that could enchant someone for a lifetime.

'Hi,' Neeti responded. She felt exposed but tried hard to cover it up by not smiling at all.

'Can we get on with the agenda without the quorum being present?' Neeti asked Shishir, in an attempt to refocus her wandering mind.

'Since we don't have a quorum, we cannot take any major decisions, but we can definitely discuss things and pass on the information to others. I am going to take minutes of the meeting anyway,' Shishir replied.

'Our order should be ready. Neeti, do you want anything to eat?' Mihir asked.

'No, thank you. I am good.'

'You should really try their *bun-maska*. It's the best!' Mihir said, folding the sleeves of his shirt.

'Okay, let me come with you, then.'

Neeti got up hesitantly, pulling up her long skirt a little bit, as her curly locks covered her face. Neeti's complexion was somewhere between wheatish and fair; it changed based on the colour of the dress she wore. Shades of browns and beige made her look wheatish, and when she wore any shades of red, she looked fair, almost pink. But today, even though she was wearing a mustard yellow dress, her cheeks turned pink as soon as she got up from the table. She wrapped the stole around her neck as she started walking. She was almost shaking as she walked and was secretly hoping that Mihir wouldn't notice it.

'Hey,' Mihir said.

'Oh, my God, he can see it,' Neeti thought.

'Neeti, *Dada* is asking what you would like to have. Shall I order a *bun-maska* for you?'

'Sure,' Neeti said, almost embarrassed for being so lost. They came back with their orders and started talking.

Shishir told Neeti that although Mihir wasn't formally a part of Prayaas, he did have informal discussions with him about most of the work they did because he respected Mihir's opinions tremendously.

'So, the plan is to pay a visit to the children of sex workers in Kamathipura next Saturday. Our focus area is improving the lives of these children through mentorship, and to help them learn, get proper education, and also enjoy their childhood,' Neeti said.

'For any project like this, the most important aspect is commitment. Visiting the children on a one-off Saturday won't really help,' Mihir remarked.

'You are right. We plan to visit the kids every Saturday, to begin with, and would meet them on a more frequent basis, depending on their needs and the availability of the volunteers. We would assign a mentor to each kid to build a strong and long-term relationship,' Neeti explained.

'We'd have to first assess the needs of the kids and establish a rapport with them over time, to make sure that they trust us enough to let us mentor them. This is going to be a gradual process, but yes, we definitely need volunteers who can commit for the long term,' Shishir added.

The discussion went well and Shishir prepared the minutes and sent them out to all the members and volunteers later that evening. Neeti came back home and could not stop thinking about Mihir. Almost a year had passed since Ruchir had broken up with her and she had never felt this way for anyone else in this past year. She did not want to get ahead of herself and left it to her feelings to determine if these were just ephemeral thoughts or if she really liked Mihir. Neeti had spent more than six months volunteering with Prayaas now. Shishir and some other members and volunteers had become her friends. Most of the information relating to the projects taken up by the NGO was exchanged online via emails and chats, and when they were not talking about work, they would discuss worldly matters.

'How are you doing?' Shishir asked Neeti one day when they were chatting online.

'I have been well, busy with work and on weekends I get to see you guys, so I can't complain. How are things with you?' Neeti responded.

'Busy with my PhD and Prayaas, of course. How are things on the personal front? Dating anyone?'

'No, not right now. I had a bitter breakup not very long ago. I don't think I am ready to date anyone yet. But recently I found a guy quite interesting.'

'Do I know him?'

'I can't tell you that.'

'I am asking this because someone I know and whom you met recently found you interesting too, so maybe I could play the matchmaker.'

'You are funny.'

'That I know. But tell me now, do I know the guy?'

'You know him very well.'

'Did you meet him at Prithvi Café?'

'Don't tell me he found me interesting. He wasn't even looking at me.'

'I guess not. Just that he told me that your mustard-coloured skirt was pretty and curly hair really suits you, and the colour of your lipstick didn't quite go with your skirt.'

'Oh, yeah? I wear the same colour, always. I mean ... what! He noticed me? You must be kidding.'

'He has asked me if he could text you. Shall I give him your phone number?'

'Well, I guess, yes.'

Neeti had no idea that Mihir had noticed her. She almost wanted to pinch herself but decided to take it easy and not behave like a giddy teenager. Next Friday evening when her cellphone beeped, she was almost certain that it would be Mihir because she had asked Shishir to pass on her phone number to him the previous Sunday. She thought that Mihir must be busy during the week and must have finally got the time to text her now. She checked the phone. The text wasn't from Mihir; it was from Sumedha, one of the members of Prayaas who was coordinating the trip to visit the children.

'We all meet at 9 a.m. at Churchgate station on Saturday,' the message read.

Neeti was rather disappointed that Mihir did not text her but did not want to dwell on it too much. After all, he was just another guy she had randomly met. She did not want to give these thoughts too much importance because she hardly knew Mihir. After the ugly breakup she had endured, she was not ready to indulge in one-sided love anymore. So, she turned off the lights and went to bed as she needed to wake up early the next day.

The next morning, she packed her bag with some snacks for the kids, water, and other essentials, and took the local train to Churchgate station. She met Sumedha there and they waited for others to arrive and then all of them headed to the venue, where they were supposed to meet the kids. It was a school building where they had reserved a few classrooms.

'Hi,' a familiar voice approached Neeti.

'Hi, I was expecting a text. I didn't know I would get to meet you in person again so soon,' Neeti said, with her eyes wide open in disbelief.

'I had made up my mind to be here today, so I thought it would make more sense to meet you rather than dropping an arid text,' Mihir explained.

'A heads-up text wouldn't have hurt.'

'I don't like all these formalities. We are here and I met you, that's all that matters.'

'But we won't have a lot of time to talk here.'

'Do you have any plans for the evening?'

'Not really.'

'I don't either.'

They met the kids. They were fifteen in all, in the age group of 3 to 14. It seemed like many people from other organizations had been meeting them, for they were at ease with the members and volunteers. Everyone played games, had food and snacks together, and then read some books. Most of the kids were comfortable reading Marathi, Hindi, and English books. Some of them recited poems and others opted to tell short stories from their textbooks.

'They all look like regular kids. I see nothing different in them,' Neeti told Sumedha.

'They are strong and resilient kids, probably have seen enough and have learnt to deal with everything at this tender age. I remember talking to one of them when I visited him at his home. He told me to come later because his mom was working at that time. He understood that her mom "worked" the way she did. He also understood that it was work because it was a means to run the household. They get mature too soon for their age, maybe with agony, as they grow up. What we need to focus on is to channel their understanding and maturity in the right direction and make sure they don't fall prey to the vultures out there due to their vulnerabilities.'

'Makes sense. I hope their lives get better soon.'

'We are here to facilitate exactly that.'

Each kid was then assigned to a volunteer to understand if the mentor–mentee system would work for them. Neeti was paired with a girl named Ananya, a shy and laconic teenager. They hugged the kids before leaving and the kids seemed to have enjoyed the company of Prayaas members and volunteers. One little girl held on to Neeti and would not let go. Neeti assured her that she would meet her again soon and, finally, the girl gave a peck on Neeti's cheek and let her go.

'I am not even wearing makeup today. This would be the strangest first date ever,' Neeti said, adjusting her *kurti* which had crumpled because she was carrying little kids around the whole day.

'You look the same with makeup too,' Mihir teased Neeti.

'You are mean.'

'Sorry, I was just kidding. Also, it's hard to believe you aren't wearing any make-up. What is this pink hue on your face?

'Aah, it's the reflection of my *kurti*.'

'Would you like to go to the movies?'

'Sure.'

***

In the theatre, Mihir watched the movie and Neeti watched Mihir.

'Did you watch the movie at all?' Mihir asked.

'Do you have two sets of eyes? Also, this is extremely embarrassing.' Neeti said, blushing so hard that the pink hue on her face was almost turning purple.

'Do you have this effect on everyone?'

'What effect?'

'Are you trying to be ignorant or you actually don't know?'

'I actually don't know.'

'Well, then I won't ruin it.'

'I am hungry. Let's try out Candy's vegetarian lasagna.'

They grabbed their lasagne and went to the open terrace area of the restaurant. The afterglow had turned the atmosphere entrancing and the ambience made it even better with fairy lights all around.

'Do you believe in love at first sight?' asked Neeti.

'Never happened with me, so can't really say.'

'Why are you so matter-of-fact?'

'What does that even mean?' Mihir said, with a smile.

'Nothing.'

'Do you believe in love at first sight?' Mihir asked Neeti.

'Well, let's head home. It's getting late,' Neeti said, not wanting to reveal too much while revealing everything through her eyes.

Mihir dropped Neeti at her place in Chembur and then proceeded to his home in Malad. The next morning Neeti woke up and was still blushing. She had her morning tea with Vandana. It was a weekend ritual.

'*Didi*, you look very happy today,' Vandana said.

'Why, don't I look happy every day?' Neeti countered.

'*Nakko re, didi*. Today it looks like a special kind of happiness.'

'All right, stop cooking stories in your head now. Come help me with the dishes here.'

Neeti quietly slipped into the bedroom and looked at herself in the mirror; she was glowing. The only problem was that gauging anything about what was going on inside Mihir's mind was impossible. He seemed almost impenetrable.

She was looking forward to the coming Saturday to attend the weekly meeting of Prayaas and was hoping that Mihir would show up there. He had not sent any texts nor had he called her after their first date. The whole week went by and still there was no communication from Mihir and she was on tenterhooks. She wanted to talk to him but wondered if it would be appropriate for her to text him when he hadn't texted after their first date. It was a Friday night, and Neeti was not a drinker, but she decided to have wine, and while she was a little disoriented, she decided to drop a text to Mihir.

'Hey, how are we doing?' Neeti wrote.

'Hey!' Mihir replied.

'Oh, so you are alive!'

'Haha, I am, just far away from Mumbai. Had to come to Singapore for training.'

'You are in Singapore?'

'Yes.'

'Does that mean I won't see you tomorrow?'

'Were we supposed to meet tomorrow?'

'No, I was hoping to catch up at the Prayaas meeting.'

'Oh, I am not officially a part of Prayaas, so I usually don't attend those meetings.'

'I know. But I was hoping.'

'Well, I can't even if I wanted to. I am too far away.'

'Come, please.'

'Hurl a stone and make me many.'

'I don't have any stones around.'

'I will see you once I'm back. By the way, as strange as it may sound, I was missing you.'

'Why didn't you text me then?'

'Because I don't.'

'Very well, then. See you when you are back.'

Mihir returned from Singapore and met Neeti the very next day. He got her a pair of earrings, a mix of yellow and white gold. She immediately wore them and the reflection of the earrings made her face glow all the more. Mihir looked at her gleaming eyes and smiled. She wanted to let him know everything she had been feeling since she saw him for the first time. 'Thanks, these are beautiful,' she managed to say, instead.

Days went by and Mihir and Neeti started meeting every weekend. During the week, Neeti was busy with work, and every Saturday morning she met her mentee, Ananya. She would go to Ananya's school and they would meet at the school premises after the classes were over. Prayaas had taken permission from the school and they had allowed Neeti to meet Ananya after all the background checks were complete. She would then go for the NGO weekly meetings and would meet Mihir immediately after that.

One Saturday night, as always, Mihir dropped Neeti home.

'Would you like to come upstairs?' Neeti asked.

'It's too late.'

'I know that.'

'You should sleep.'

'I don't want to.'

'Neeti, it's really late. Go upstairs. We will talk tomorrow.'

'I want to talk today.'

Mihir looked into Neeti's eyes, held her hand, and walked to her apartment on the second floor.

'I would have guessed that it's your apartment.'

'How so?'

'It smells of you.'

'Would you like some tea?'

'We won't be able to sleep if we had tea now.'

'Do you want to sleep?'

They both smiled at each other. Mihir then held Neeti's face in his palms and kissed her. She closed her eyes; she wanted to remember this moment for the rest of her life. He then took her in his arms and carried her to the bed. She kept staring at him.

'Sleep, now,' Mihir said.

'Would you sleep with me?'

'Neeti, sleep now. Please.'

'Okay.'

Neeti hugged Mihir. He held her tight, kissing her gently. Both of them wanted to take things slow. They liked each other but did not want to rush things. They continued meeting over the weekends and kept in regular touch during weekdays.

'Hey, we are going to watch the IPL match at Wankhede Stadium. Would you like to join us?' Mihir asked.

'Sure, it sounds fun,' Neeti replied.

Mihir introduced Neeti to a couple of friends and they discussed the logistics for the day. They also prepared T-shirts supporting the Mumbai Indians team. After the match, all of them had coffee together. They chatted for some time and then called it a day. Neeti and Mihir decided to go for a walk.

'Would you like to go to Bandstand with me?' Neeti asked.

'Sure. But why Bandstand? We are at Churchgate, we can go to Bade Miyaan's. Their food is to die for,' Mihir insisted.

'All right, let's go to Bade Miyaan's, but promise me you would go to Bandstand with me soon.'

'I will, but what's the matter?'

'I have to erase some memories, and the best way to do so is to create better ones.'

'Sure, but right now I want to erase the hunger pangs inside my stomach. Let's go to Bade Miyaan's.'

They reached the place and it was packed. They waded through the crowd to the cash counter and placed their order. Luckily, some people were leaving and they managed to grab two plastic chairs and a small table. Most people weren't so lucky, they either had to stand and eat, or they walked up to their cars that were parked on both sides of the road and had their food inside their cars. There was loud and upbeat music playing in most people's cars and everyone seemed to be enjoying the evening.

'How did I not know about this place yet?' Neeti exclaimed.

'You didn't know about many awesome things before meeting me.'

'Get over yourself!'

'All right, let's eat. I'm starving.'

A few days later they went to the Bandstand promenade and took a walk before settling on a rock alongside the sea. Both of them were looking constantly at the sea and didn't speak for long before they realized that they had forgotten to talk to each other. There was strange comfort in this silence and neither of the two wanted to ruin it by talking.

'Do you know you get the best greasy vegetarian manchurian here?' Mihir said finally, as he laughed out loud.

'What? Are you serious? I have been coming to Bandstand for as long as I can remember. How do I not know about this place?'

'As I said before, you didn't know about many awesome things before meeting me.'

'They sound awful, but I've got to try them now.'

'Let's go then,' Mihir said as he took Neeti's hand in his.

Neeti had the greasy manchurian and could not stop laughing. It was salty and greasy but strangely addictive.

'I don't believe I just had the world's best worst dish,' Neeti was in stitches.

Mihir placed his arm around Neeti as they left the place. Mihir's cologne was now a familiar smell that Neeti not only recognized but also craved for. It was a beautiful summer evening and the sun had not yet set, so they decided to go for a walk on the other side of Bandra Reclamation. The pathway was uneven and also had some gravel scattered all around which made it difficult for Neeti to walk, even though she was wearing flats. Mihir held her hand as she struggled to walk. She looked at him and saw his eyes shining brightly. The sky had turned orange and she could see its reflection in his eyes. She wanted to capture this in her memory forever. They saw the sunset together. Slowly the sky started turning pink and, in a few moments, there was a medley of pink, orange, and turquoise in the sky.

'Why do you like me?' Neeti asked.

'Honestly, I don't know. I haven't felt this way about anyone in a long time. After my breakup a few years ago, I had given up hope to finding love. But after meeting you, I realized that love doesn't always hurt. In fact, I think love should never hurt. If it hurts, how can it be love? I feel happy when I am with you, I can be myself with you. I don't feel this way with many people.'

'Why do you like me?' he added.

'I feel that I have known you for a long time. I feel safe with you, and I haven't felt this comfortable with anyone ever before. You let me be me, I don't need any filters or masks when I am with you.'

'Do you believe in love?' Mihir asked.

'I used to, but then had a bitter breakup. I don't know what to believe in anymore. What we think of love, is just fleeting happiness which disappears, leaving behind pain and scars.'

'Do you want to talk about it?'

'Let's talk about us.'

'Are you sure this isn't a rebound?'

'If it doesn't stand the test of time, I will know that it's a rebound. If it does, then you will have your answer. I just want to make sure that nobody is hurt this time.'

'I can wait for my entire lifetime. I hope that's enough time to figure it out.'

'That was *filmy*!' Neeti burst out laughing.

'Are the old memories erased now?'

'I don't care anymore.'

Mihir and Neeti met at Prithvi Café, their favourite spot even on weekdays now. They sat on the same side of the table and held hands. Life seemed perfect to Neeti, she had a fulfilling work life, she was volunteering for a noble cause and post-work she got to meet the most amazing man she had ever known.

'I am applying to universities in the US,' Mihir told Neeti one fine day.

'Wait, what?' Neeti tried processing what Mihir had just said.

'I want to get a PhD and get into academia.'

'Slow down. Where did this come from?'

'I have been thinking about this for a long time, and I met some people in Singapore, even they suggested that I should look at schools in the US for my PhD.'

'Can't you do that from India? I know Shishir is getting his PhD from a university in Mumbai.'

'No, the kind of research I want to do, I would need to go to the US. I have identified some schools I am going to apply to.'

'And you will come back after completing your PhD, right?

'I am not sure, Neeti.'

'I don't understand this. What are you not sure of?' Neeti got up from the chair.

'Don't get worked up. I haven't even started applying to schools yet. Calm down!'

'I need to know what you are planning to do. How long will it take you to complete your PhD?'

'It will take me at least five years. It can take more.'

Neeti went silent. She sat back on the chair, looked away and sighed heavily.

'Look at me, Neeti, please.'

'What about us?'

'We will be fine. I said calm down,' Mihir said, holding Neeti's face in his palms.

She didn't speak a word after that. He dropped her home and they didn't talk to each other for a couple of days, and then Mihir texted her, 'It's not going to be as bad as you think it would be.'

'Okay,' she replied.

'Please trust me. If you behave like this, it would be difficult for me to focus on my applications.'

'I trust you, and I don't mean to put you under any pressure. It's just that I didn't have an inkling about your aspirations to study and settle down in the US.'

3

The Decision

Neeti was still trying to come to terms with what Mihir had recently told her. She did not want to put him under any stress but at the same time wanted some clarity about her future. Although she thought it was premature to ruminate too much about it right now, she wanted to be prepared for what was coming her way. Without being too aggressive, Neeti did bring it up every time they met and Mihir assured her every time that they would be able to handle the situation and that she needed to relax. Mihir's assurances worked but only partially. A part of Neeti was not able to accept that Mihir would be leaving soon and would be away for five long years, or probably even more. One day after Neeti came back home from work, her phone rang. It was Rhea.

'Hi, Rhea. How have you been?' Neeti was excited.

'I have been well, busy with work and home. I have some news for you.'

'I have some news for you too, but you tell me first.'

'I am pregnant!'

'Oh my God! Congratulations! I am going to be an aunt! This is awesome! When is the due date?'

'In March. Now your turn.'

'I have someone in my life.'

'Are you serious? This is some news. Tell me everything. It's been ages since we last talked at length!'

'Yeah, I figured you must be busy so didn't want to disturb you.'

'What kind of nonsense is this? So many people ping me for no reason and then have nothing to talk about after exchanging pleasantries, and you are at the other end of the spectrum. You did not ping me even once after getting into a full-fledged relationship! Anyway, now tell me who the lucky guy is.'

'Lucky or unlucky, only time will tell. I met him through the NGO folks I told you about the last time we talked. His name is Mihir.'

'This is so exciting! I am really happy for you.'

'Yes, I am pretty positive about him too.'

'When did this happen? What all have you guys done? Has he proposed to you yet? Tell me every single detail. And send me his picture!'

'Whoa! So many questions!'

'Yes, I am super excited for you!'

'I met him at Prithvi Café about a year ago and we hit it off immediately. There was some kind of pull that I felt the moment I saw him, and the same happened with him too. He has not proposed to me yet, but we both know in our heart of hearts that we want to be together forever.'

'This is wonderful. What does he do?'

'He is a physical therapist and is going to pursue his PhD in the US. He has started applying to universities there.'

'Oh, so you guys will see how it goes as a long-distance relationship and will decide everything once he is back?'

'He doesn't plan on coming back.'

'Have you thought this through? You love your work and your life in Mumbai. Are you sure you would be okay leaving everything and settling down in a place you have little idea about?'

'We haven't discussed these things in detail yet.'

'Well ... then you should.'

'I will.'

'I have seen you heartbroken once. Just make sure this time you know for sure what you are getting yourself into.'

'I also don't want to get hurt again, but being cynical also would not help.'

'I'm not asking you to be cynical, I am just asking you to be cautious.'

***

Mihir got busy submitting applications to the universities and Neeti didn't feel that it was the best time to discuss her future in the US. He needed to secure his future first and it felt ill-timed to even bring it up. They continued to meet on the weekends.

'I feel like you are sitting right next to me and are still missing me. Cheer up, Neeti. We need to make the most of our time together. Once I move to the US, we will have a long-distance relationship anyway. Please don't make me feel like I am not there with you even now. You are so close to me yet so distant,' Mihir said, not mincing words.

'I don't want to lose you.'

'Nobody is going to lose anyone. No matter where I am physically, I will always be with you. You are the one for me and I hope I am the one for you.'

'You are, but the very thought that you are going to be away for a long time makes me wonder if we will be able to sustain this.'

'I'm sure about you. I am going there so that we can have a better future. You need to trust me, Neeti.'

'I trust you. it was just too unexpected for me. I had imagined our life together in Mumbai.'

'I'm sorry this came as a surprise to you. I wish I had started attending Prayaas meetings earlier, or we had met earlier. All my close friends knew about my aspirations. I just never got a chance to talk to you about them before. Maybe I should have.'

'I'm sorry if I am making it harder for you. I will try to calm down and not make a big deal about it.'

'I am not trying to make you feel bad about how you are feeling, Neeti. But this has been my dream and I am so close to realizing it. I want you to be a part of my journey. Don't make me feel so distant.'

In a few months' time, the responses to Mihir's applications started coming in. He got accepted to the university that was first on the list of his preference and he was thrilled. He called Neeti as soon as he read the acceptance email. She congratulated him and said that they should meet and celebrate his achievement.

They met at Prithvi Café that evening and Neeti brought Mihir flowers, hugged him, and congratulated him again.

'You look pale, Neeti. Are you still overthinking about me moving away?' Mihir asked.

'No, it's just the reflection of my white *kurti*,' Neeti made a failed attempt to cover up. She was, in fact, upset that he would be leaving soon. She wanted to discuss their future together but didn't want to be a wet blanket and tried her best to celebrate his admission to his dream university.

When the time for Mihir to leave got closer, Neeti and Shishir arranged a farewell party for him at Prithvi Café with the entire Prayaas team. Everyone congratulated Mihir at this huge milestone in his academic and professional journey.

Neeti tried to put all negative thoughts at bay and did her best to be involved in the preparations for Mihir's big move. The next few days were spent making several lists of the things Mihir would need in the US, shopping for essentials, and packing bags. Since Kansas City got freezing cold in winter and Mihir had lived in Mumbai all his life, they made sure they bought enough warm clothes to get him through the first fall / winter. If he needed more, he could buy them from Kansas City after settling in there. With countless things to remember and plenty of stuff to pack, days went by at a rate of knots and it was time for Mihir to finally leave.

'We will do video chats on the weekends, don't worry. It's just a matter of few years,' Mihir said.

'Just a matter of few years…' Neeti repeated and grimaced.

'Don't do this to me, it will get really hard for me to leave like this.'

'I will miss you,' she said, fighting her tears, and hugged him.

'I will miss you too, but I know we can handle this,' Mihir said, hugging Neeti tight.

She went to the airport to see him off. She was excited about a new phase in Mihir's professional journey, but somewhere in her heart she also had a fear of losing him. It was going to be a long-distance relationship for an extended period of time and she was also not sure about what the future held in store for them.

Mihir texted Neeti once he reached Kansas City and told her that he liked the place and would soon move into an apartment that he had booked online. He got busy with his classes, lab, and also in the process of settling down in a new city. For the initial few days, there were no phone calls, only texts. The time zone difference made it challenging for them to talk over the phone the way they used to in India, so they decided that they would talk over the phone or video chat only on the weekends and would keep in touch via texts at other times.

Neeti decided to focus completely on work and take a leap of faith when it came to her relationship with Mihir. She got another promotion and was now an assistant general manager. Mihir was working laboriously towards completing his PhD as soon as he possibly could, so he would spend even the weekends in the lab. He was learning about a different culture and was spending time familiarizing himself with the place and the people. The weekend calls became sporadic, but he made sure to drop a text when he couldn't call her.

Neeti was still spending her weekends volunteering for Prayaas and would hang out with that group most weekends after the meeting.

'How are things?' Shishir asked Neeti.

'Pretty good.'

'You want to grab a cup of coffee after the meeting?'

'Sure.'

Shishir and Neeti went to a coffee shop in Juhu and he offered to place the order.

'A regular cappuccino with honey on the side?' Shishir asked.

'How do you know this?'

'Don't underestimate my observation skills. We've gone out to have coffee with the group enough number of times to know this,' he placed the order and chose to sit on the same side as Neeti.

'You seem to be in low spirits. Is everything all right? I can imagine with Mihir being away it must be a little lonely, but we all are here for you. You know that, right?'

'Thanks, Shishir, it means a lot. But I'm not lonely. Work keeps me busy, and then I have my mentee to take care of on the weekends. We also have these weekend meetings where I get to meet all of you. So, I am doing all right, but I won't deny, I miss Mihir.'

'Is he visiting India anytime soon? I'm finding it hard these days to catch up with him because of the difference in time zones.'

'No, I don't think he would be visiting India anytime soon. He needs to take care of his coursework and experiments.'

'Understandable, but just wanted to remind you that we are there. I'm just a phone call away if you ever need to talk.'

'Thanks, Shishir.'

Neeti was now supervising new hires at work and Shekhar had asked the head of the department to let Neeti work in his team permanently. She was flourishing under his mentorship and Shekhar was delighted to see her take up more responsibilities at work. Neeti continued to visit Ananya at her school every Saturday morning and was pleased to see the progress she was making.

'It is a wonderful feeling to see Ananya gaining ground. From being a shy teen to becoming a confident young adult, she has definitely exceeded my expectations. She is thriving in academics and has started participating in extra-curricular activities too,' Neeti told Shishir one Saturday evening after the Prayaas meeting.

'That's exactly what mentorship does to you. I am glad that the dream I saw a few years ago is becoming a reality now, all thanks to Prayaas members and volunteers like you.'

'The pleasure is all mine. All this gives me a purpose. I know what I do during the week also helps people indirectly but this way I know for sure that I am making a difference in someone's life and it gives me immense satisfaction and hope.'

'I feel grateful that all this is working out really well.'

Neeti reached for her bag that was on the other side of the table. Shishir handed it to her, and when she was about to leave, he asked, 'What are you doing this evening?'

'Nothing much. I was planning to go home and watch something on TV.'

'Would you like to go someplace for dinner?'

'I have some leftovers at home.'

'I know a very nice pizza place. You can have the leftovers tomorrow.'

'Okay, let's go.'

The live music at the restaurant made Neeti miss Mihir, but she didn't want to spoil the evening for Shishir, so she tried her best to hide her emotions and enjoy the music and the evening.

'I wanted to say something to you,' Shishir said.

'Don't. You are a friend and I want you to remain my friend, please,' Neeti snapped back. She had been observing Shishir for some time and he also had been making it too obvious for her to figure out how he felt about her.

'Mihir is not going to come back to India. I recently had a chat with him. He wants to pursue his research dreams and he is exactly where he can make them come true. He will not look back now.'

'I know that, and that changes nothing for me.'

'Are you going to wait for him until he finishes his PhD?'

'Nobody is waiting for anyone. Mihir and I are in a relationship.'

'And what happens after he finishes his PhD? Are you going to leave all this—your job, your friends, family, everything—and move to the US? For all you know, he is not coming back!'

'I repeat, that changes nothing. I love him and I will be with him no matter what,' Neeti said, this time more firmly so as to put the point across loud and clear.

'He is pursuing his dreams and you are pursuing him. Get out of your bubble and see the reality screaming so loud in your face!'

'You are hurting me, Shishir. Being Mihir's best friend, you know very well how much we love each other. You also know that he had had these dreams of being a researcher for a long time, even before he met me. He never kept me in the dark. I can't believe instead of supporting us, you are trying to poison my mind against him.'

'I'm sorry, Neeti. But it hurts to see you like this. I've liked you since the first time we met, and then Mihir came along. I never thought my feelings were so strong for you until he left India, and I saw you missing him every single time I met you after that. I can't see you like this. All I want is to see you happy.'

'Thanks, Shishir but Mihir is the one for me. I have made my decision.'

'Okay, I don't want to sound too pushy, but if you ever change your mind, let me know.'

'Shishir, you are a great guy and I have tremendous amount of respect for you and Prayaas, but I don't have feelings for you. I wish I did. It would have made life much easier for me. But please don't make it any more difficult for me. You are a friend, and a friend that I really need.'

After that day, Shishir did not bring it up ever again and Neeti was much relieved. They both were mature and didn't let this bring any awkwardness to the great friendship they shared. After the initial hiccups, the feeling that Mihir won't be around for a long time was sinking in, and Neeti and Mihir were trying to work out the best way to keep in touch through phone calls and video chats, despite the difference in the time zones.

'Why don't you come over for a few days?' Mihir asked one day.

'I would love to. I have a visitor visa already because I visited DC for training soon after I was hired, so I can literally just get a ticket, pack my bags and visit you. Why did we not think about it earlier?' Neeti said excitedly.

'Well, we have thought about it now, so let's do it.'

Neeti visited Mihir in Kansas City and he was excited to see her at the airport. He had brought her flowers and she was finally at peace seeing him in front of her eyes. She was tired of those video calls and had craved for Mihir's touch far too long.

'You've grown up so much!' Mihir teased Neeti.

'Stop it, give me a hug!' Neeti cried. They hugged and then went to his place. He had rented an apartment close to the university. Mihir gave her a tour of the apartment. It was a rather large studio apartment and one could tell that it was a bachelor's pad. He carried her in his arms and kissed her halfway through the tour. He wanted to hold her like this forever.

'It's surreal to have you in my apartment. I can imagine how it would feel like once we are married.'

'We are not living in a bachelor's pad! Speaking of which, let me arrange some of the stuff for you.'

'You are here only for four days. You can't be spending your time doing all this!'

'What should I spend my time doing then?'

'This,' Mihir said as he kissed her again.

They spent almost the whole night talking and catching up on things that they didn't get to discuss over the phone. Neeti didn't let go of Mihir even for a second and finally slept in his arms. The next morning, Mihir took Neeti to his university.

The campus was colossal and it took them the whole day to cover its entirety. After taking permission from his supervisor, Mihir took Neeti to his lab. There were microscopes, freezers, incubators, and reagent bottles all around. There were quail eggs in the incubator and tiny embryos were growing on cell culture plates. Mihir then placed one of the embryos under the microscope and showed it to Neeti. She saw the state-of-the-art equipment in the lab and understood why he wanted to do his research in this lab.

They spent the next two days exploring the city and Mihir tried to gauge if Neeti was feeling any connect with the place. But Neeti's eyes were fixated only on Mihir; she had not seen him for a long time and after these couple of days, she was not sure when she would see him again, so she didn't want to waste even a fraction of a second not focusing on him. They came back home later that evening, and sat in the living area and talked for some time.

'I can't believe you would be leaving tomorrow morning.'

'Four days flew by.'

'They did. I wish you could stay here with me forever. I will miss you.'

'We will talk over the phone, and will do video chats.'

'I don't think those will help anymore.'

'I know, but that's what we can do, at least for the near future.'

'Do you want to get married and come over here permanently?'

'You need to focus on your PhD. I just want you to be there for me, and I'll be fine.'

'I'm sorry it's harder than I thought it would be. Do you think we can sustain this for four more years?'

'I can wait even for ten, if you have any doubts, you tell me now.'

'Are you kidding me? I have everything I had ever desired, I am working in my dream lab, and I have a woman who supports me despite me being miles apart. I may not express it often but I love you more than you can ever imagine. I know I'm not able to make much time for you these days but there is not a single day when I don't think about you. You complete my world.'

Mihir then held Neeti's hand and looked into her eyes. He kissed her and let her know she was the only one he wanted to be with. He drove her to the airport the next morning and she boarded the flight with a heavy heart. She had thought this trip would help but she missed Mihir all the more after spending four days with him.

'Reached?' Mihir texted Neeti.

'Yes, the aircraft just landed. We are still taxiing.'

'So, how did you like Kansas City?'

'Different from what I had imagined about the US in general. I had visited DC for my training and Kansas City and DC are poles apart.'

'Yes, life in the Midwest is different and slow paced. Are you up for a slow-paced life?'

'I am up for a life with you. I haven't really thought of the pace yet.'

'I will try my best to move from the Midwest to a fast-paced place.'

'I will be fine, don't stress about it.'

'I need to, I will not be the one leaving my job, family, and friends after marriage, you would be. This is the least I can do—to make you feel as comfortable as I possibly can. Are you sure about this?'

'I am sure about you, that's all that matters.'

Neeti and Mihir continued to do their weekly video chats and talked to each other every night. They both were focusing on their careers for now and knew that they were going to be together one day, and that kept them going.

One Saturday morning, during their usual chit-chat session over tea, Vandana asked Neeti, '*Didi*, how did you like America?'

'It was good,' Neeti replied.

'You are going to live in America now?'

'Maybe.'

'I have heard you don't get any house helps there.'

'That's correct. I will take you with me.'

'*Didi*, stop kidding. How will you do all the household work?'

'I know how to do the household work. If needed I can do it, and Mihir will help me as well.'

'I wish I could go with you.'

'You are such a sweetheart. I don't know what I did to deserve you.'

'I feel the same way about you, *didi*. I never felt I was a house help. You have always treated me like a sister. I will really miss you if you leave Mumbai.'

'I will miss you too. But I am not leaving anytime soon. It will take a few years.'

Neeti's office had moved from Nariman Point to Bandra Kurla Complex now. She was living in the company-provided apartment in Chembur like before, but would now take auto-rickshaw to commute to the office. There was an auto-rickshaw driver who would come at the same time every morning to pick her up, so she hired him on a monthly basis. It made life easier for her as she would not have to look for auto-rickshaws in the morning and provided the auto-rickshaw driver a confirmed customer every day. One morning while taking Neeti to work, the auto-rickshaw driver asked, 'Madam, can I ask you a question?'

'Sure,' Neeti replied as she wore her work ID around her neck.

'What do people keep doing inside these big buildings every day?'

Neeti appreciated the sneaky profoundness in the presumably innocuous question. She wondered what exactly people did inside these tall buildings. Was it any different from what the auto-rickshaw driver was doing?

'What do you think they do?' she asked the auto-rickshaw driver.

'They keep writing something on their computers all day.'

'Just like you drive this auto-rickshaw, someone needs to drive companies, banks, hospitals, etc. It's similar to what you do, just different in some ways,' Neeti smiled.

'*Haan*, madam, you are right. Just like I drive the auto-rickshaw, my wife drives the household, everyone is responsible for driving something or the other. Just the ways of doing those things take different shapes and forms.'

'Absolutely!'

***

Two years had passed since Neeti visited Mihir. They were still together, thankfully.

It was a Friday night and Neeti got a text. 'You need to come to my place tomorrow. I know it's your birthday but since you didn't invite me, I invited myself and some others too to celebrate your special day,' it read.

'No, Shishir, I am in no mood to celebrate my birthday. We aren't kids anymore,' Neeti replied.

'Come on, Neeti. Be a sport! I assure you it will be worth it.'

The next morning Neeti woke up early and made *sooji halwa* and did a little *pooja* at home.

'Happy birthday, *didi*!' Vandana said cheerfully.

'Thank you, Vandana,' Neeti replied.

'I got you something.'

'You didn't have to do it. What is it?'

'Open it and see.'

'They are not expensive like the ones Mihir *bhaiya* had got for you, but I am sure they will look really good on you.'

'These earrings are beautiful. One of my friends is throwing a party for me today, I will wear these to the party.'

'You will wear these to your party? They aren't very expensive, *didi*.'

'They are precious! Come let's have tea now. I've also made *halwa*. I want you to have some and take some for your daughter as well.'

Neeti got ready for the party in the evening and wore the earrings that Vandana had gifted her. They were light blue flowers with white alternate petals and a hint of silver. They matched perfectly with her light blue georgette maxi dress. Mihir had not wished her on her birthday and she was slightly upset about it, but thought he might be busy. She reached Shishir's place and Sumedha and other members and volunteers of Prayaas were also there. They all wished her, and Shishir then brought out her birthday cake. They turned off the lights and everyone went quiet. There was pin-drop silence and Neeti heard light footsteps approaching her, and then a familiar voice wished her 'happy birthday'. Shishir turned the lights on, and Mihir gave Neeti a hug. She was overjoyed and hugged Mihir back and thanked Shishir for the best birthday gift ever.

'You are here…' Neeti said softly.

'I am,' Mihir kissed her forehead.

'I thought you forgot my birthday.'

'How could I?'

Mihir spent two weeks in Mumbai and made the most of his time with Neeti. They went to all the places they had not been to for the last two years. They made another trip to Bandstand and Neeti wouldn't let go of Mihir's hand this time even for a minute.

'Take care of yourself, and trust me, we will be together very soon,' Mihir said, as he walked towards the security check-in at the airport. Mihir worked day and night and was able to complete his PhD in four-and-a-half years. He visited India once again during this period and Neeti also went to see Mihir. They both held on to the love they had for each other during this entire period.

'I'm defending my thesis tomorrow, wish me luck. I wish you were here,' Mihir said with a bright smile on a video chat with Neeti.

'I wish I could be there, but my current investigation is time-sensitive and I can't take any days off from work right now. I just want to let you know that I am immensely proud of you and everything you have achieved. All the very best!' Neeti said cheerfully.

Mihir successfully defended his thesis and sent Neeti pics of his graduation in real-time. She congratulated him and was over the moon because not only did this mean that Mihir had graduated but it also meant that finally, they would be together soon.

Long-distance relationships are not the easiest to deal with, but once you are sure of the person, you make it work, come hell or high water. There were good days and then there were bad, but at the end of this long period, they were still together. They knew it was time for them to take the next step. So, they got their families involved in the conversations relating to engagement and wedding. It was going to be a big decision, especially because Neeti would have to move to a different country and leave her job, her family, and friends, and would have to start a new life from scratch.

Neeti started packing her belongings in Mumbai; it was now time to leave the place she had revered so much. Mumbai gave Neeti her identity, her professional successes, a mentor for life, and friends that she was more than thankful for. Her heart was heavier than the bags that she and Vandana had finally packed.

'Make sure you continue your daughter's education and take care of yourself. I will miss you a lot. You were never a domestic help, you were a sister and I hope you know that,' Neeti told Vandana as she handed some money to her.

'*Didi*, you are calling me sister and also saying that I *was* a sister. I will be your sister forever. My daughter has opened a Facebook account for me, you add me as a friend there, and I will keep in touch with you there. I will also send you my daughter's school graduation pictures. I will add this money to the amount I'm saving to buy a new computer for my daughter.'

'I had completely forgotten that your daughter is computer savvy. I will add you on Facebook. I hardly use it but I will log in from now on. You don't have to wait to buy a computer for your daughter, Neeti said, as she went inside her bedroom and came back with some more money and handed it to Vandana.'

'No, *didi*. I will get it in some time. Why are you spending so much money on it?'

'Take this as a parting gift from me.'

'Thank you, *didi*. You will make me cry now!'

Before leaving, Neeti met Shishir and the whole team of Prayaas. Her office also arranged a farewell party for her. She had decided to take a long leave for now and had not resigned yet, but everyone in the office was almost certain that she would not return once she moved to the US. Neeti hugged

Shekhar and thanked him for shaping her into the professional she was exceedingly proud of becoming.

'Keep in touch and always remember that I am just a phone call away,' Shekhar told Neeti.

She spent the last two evenings before leaving Mumbai at Marine Drive and Bandstand. It had still not sunk in that she was leaving the city she connected with more than the place she grew up in. She collected small pieces of rock from both the sites and packed them in her luggage. As she placed a lock outside her apartment door, she felt a lump in her throat. She took a deep breath and took a cab to the airport. She rolled down the window of the cab to soak in the familiar smell and feel of Mumbai for the last time to engrave them in her memory forever.

4

The Dilemma

Neeti reached her parents' home in Dehradun and planned out all the details of the wedding with her parents, Aanandi and Aseem. But the question that was lurking in her and also their minds was whether she would be able to give up her career that she had painstakingly built. One day, after she and also her parents came back home after shopping for her wedding *lehenga*, Neeti looked at her parents and her entire professional journey started running in her head. It was almost eight years ago, when Neeti had this conversation with her dad in Mumbai.

'What would you like to eat?' Aseem asked.

'I could have answered that question about independent directors better. Besides, I was wearing a georgette *salwar kameez*. I should have worn cotton. It was an interview for a government job, after all,' Neeti thought to herself.

'I am not hungry,' she said.

Neeti was too disappointed in herself to feel hungry. The question she was asked during the interview was stuck in her head and she knew that she had a better answer than what she gave out. Aseem was persistent to feed Neeti something. He knew she was tired and hungry. She had gone for her interview straight from the railway station after a day-long journey. The only thing she had had in the morning, at around 8 a.m. was a glass of mixed fruit juice from a street vendor right outside the office where the interview was scheduled to be held, that too after much coaxing from him. Neeti didn't want to stuff herself too much because she did not want to feel sleepy during the interview, but Aseem told her that she would probably pass out if she didn't have anything at all. Finally, she gave in and had had that glass of juice. She was supposed to reach the venue by 8.30 a.m. and they were there at 8.15 a.m. They waited at the reception area until her name was called out. All the candidates were divided into groups of eight or nine and each group was assigned to a particular interview panel. Her group was asked to head over to the waiting area outside a conference room, where they waited for their turn. The interview was to take place in the conference room.

'I cleared my civil services preliminary exam and I am waiting for the results of the mains to come out. In the meantime, I thought I would take this exam and see how this plays out,' one of the candidates from Neeti's group said.

'I have my RBI interview scheduled soon. I will probably then decide which one to choose out of these two,' said another.

All the candidates in Neeti's group were sitting in a circle for some reason. She was trying to understand why these people were talking about the things they were talking about, rather than just letting people relax before the interview. She never liked small talks, and small talks blowing your own trumpet were an absolute turnoff for her. She got up and went to the window and looked out. She could see Marine Drive from there, and it calmed her down. She continued standing there until she was called for her turn at around noon, and the interview lasted for about 25 minutes. Her interview panel had three members and each of them asked her two questions. Neeti answered all of them and just when she thanked everyone for the opportunity and stood up to leave the room, one of the members of the panel asked her another question: 'Thousands of potential candidates took the written test across the country. Hundreds of them got called for the interview. There are a total of 70 vacant positions and after accounting for the reserved quota for the SC, ST, and OBC categories, there are about 25 slots available for the General category. Aren't you apprehensive that you may not get a spot?'

'Sir, I just need one slot, and as long as that one slot is available, there is every possibility that I can make it,' Neeti responded.

'Thanks, Neeti. That would be all.'

'Thank you, sir.'

Aseem was waiting for Neeti at the reception area and the moment she came out, he could tell that Neeti was not entirely pleased with her performance. But he also knew that she was always too hard on herself, so probably she did better than she thought she did.

Neeti said she was not hungry but he knew she was upset.

'Would you like some ice cream, then?' Aseem asked, knowing very well how much she loved ice cream.

'Yes!'

'Okay, we will get you ice cream, but please for my sake have some food first.'

'But I am not hungry.'

'I'm your dad, Neeti, I know you better than you know yourself.'

'All right, let's have some *pav-bhaaji* downstairs.'

They had *pav-bhaaji* and ice cream, visited Hanging Gardens, got an instant picture clicked by a local photographer carrying a Polaroid camera, and took the train back home.

Neeti had no hopes of clearing the interview and yet was secretly hoping to receive the offer letter in the mail. She was convinced that it was her georgette *salwar kameez* that was the deal-breaker. She was an amusing mix of intelligence, perseverance, and such quirky thoughts. She kept thinking about it and waited every day for the postman to come with the results of the interview in the mail.

The postman wore the typical uniform that you see in movies, with the only exception that he did not wear the cap. He was a friendly guy, but spoke very little and only when required. He rode a black Atlas bicycle and rang its bell whenever he reached the gate of any home where he needed to deliver mail. For Neeti, it was almost a ritual at around noon every day to go to the verandah the moment she heard the sound of the bicycle bell. The neighbourhood had ten houses in a row, five on either side. Neeti's house was the last one on the right. Some days she would get out on the lane when the postman reached the first house, and then he would hand over the mail to Neeti instead of dropping it in the mailbox.

That day she was extremely anxious. She came out to the verandah at her usual time, without even hearing the bicycle bell, and there was no sign of the postman. She roamed around the neighbourhood for a while and came back. Aanandi was making *rajma* and had already cut onions and tomatoes by then. Neeti was fond of cooking and loved cooking the *masala*. That was her favourite pastime at home. Cooking the *masala* meant sautéing chopped onions and tomatoes in oil with spices to make a smooth paste. The onions had turned golden brown and it was time to add tomatoes. Exactly then, Neeti heard the sound of the bicycle bell. 'I have added tomatoes to the onions, Maa, and have reduced the flame of the burner, the *masala* won't burn. I will be back in a moment,' Neeti screamed and rushed outside to fetch the mail.

'It's a letter from the government. If it's some good news, I want *baksheesh*,' the postman said with the sweetest smile ever, as he handed over a brown sealed envelope to Neeti.

'Let me first open the envelope,' Neeti said as her heart started racing. The postman waited patiently outside the house as she ran inside, visibly shaking. She placed the letter in the temple inside their home, said a quick prayer, and opened the envelope.

'Are you okay?' Aanandi enquired, stirring the *masala*.

'I don't know,' Neeti said, with a tear rolling down her cheek. She had almost given up hopes on her chances of making it through the interview. But the heart has a mind of its own; it never stops desiring the seemingly impossible. Her heart had won. She had cleared the interview.

'CONGRATULATIONS!' the letter read.

'I cleared the interview, Maa!' Neeti announced excitedly.

'Congratulations, little one! Now you understand that it's not what you wear that matters, it's what you know and speak that does.'

'Yes, I do.'

Aanandi kissed Neeti on her forehead and then hugged her. Neeti still had the envelope in her hand and as she stood in front of Aanandi, numb for about twenty seconds when she realized that the postman was waiting at the gate. She asked Aanandi for some money for the postman's *baksheesh* and went outside where he was still waiting patiently. After getting blessings from the postman, Neeti came back inside, beaming ear to ear, her eyes still wet, shining brightly.

Neeti immediately called Aseem and broke the big news to him. She had never desired a government job and was only hoping to get a private corporate job, she wanted to give everything a try. She was too young to even understand what it meant to have a government job in India. She only wanted to use her education and training, and earn a living.

The organization that Neeti was going to work for was an autonomous body regulating the stock markets in India, and it was in the news on TV daily, just like the National Stock Exchange and Bombay Stock Exchange. Neeti had read so much about the organization in her textbooks, newspapers, and magazines, that it was almost surreal for her to imagine herself working for the same organization. She was ready to begin her professional life. Her first posting was Mumbai, where she would start as a trainee officer on probation for six months and then would get the designation of manager. This was Neeti's first real job and she was in her early twenties. She was going to be a manager soon. she was overwhelmed and exhilarated. She had exactly three months to pack her bags with all the things she would need to start a new life, get ready for her big move, and prepare her heart to leave her parents and her hometown to pursue her dreams in a city she had never lived in before.

A part of her was nervous but it was soon overtaken by excitement. However, the fact that she would now be living independently away from home and family was something she was still trying to come to terms with. On the day she was leaving, Aanandi gave Neeti a mini *Hanuman Chalisa* to always keep in her wallet.

'This will protect you,' Aanandi said as she hugged Neeti, with tears in her eyes.

'Wait, give me a minute,' Neeti said.

'What happened?'

'Let me just go inside quickly and come back.'

'Is everything okay?'

'Give me a minute,' Neeti ran inside and came back quickly.

'What is it?'

'I had forgotten to take the picture that Papa and I got clicked in Mumbai when we had gone there for my interview.'

'Let's go, Neeti. We are getting late,' Aseem said, waiting for Neeti in the cab. He was going to Mumbai with Neeti to help her settle down at her new abode.

'Coming, Papa.'

***

'Neeti, are you okay?' Aseem asked, bringing Neeti back to the present.

'I'm fine. Am I doing the right thing?' Neeti asked, in response.

'What does your heart say?'

'My heart lies where Mihir is.'

'Then don't have second thoughts, go with what your heart says is right.'

Both the families decided to keep the engagement right before the wedding so that Mihir would need to fly to India only once. All the details were worked out between the families and everyone seemed pleased with the arrangements.

'I am getting married,' Neeti told Rhea.

'No way!'

'I don't believe it myself.'

'When is the wedding?'

'January 5th.'

'Very close to my delivery date. I wish you had chosen another date. Or maybe I should not have chosen to get pregnant again at this time!'

'You are still the same! The priest decided the date.'

'Have you decided about leaving your job and what you plan to do there?'

'I am taking a long leave for now, just giving myself some more time to think about it, although I have made up my mind to resign from the job. I have done some basic research online on what kind of options I have. I will have to be on a spouse-dependent visa, to begin with, and I would not be able to work. I will try to be a homemaker, at least for the near future.'

'Are you sure about this?'

'I am sure about Mihir, that's all I know.'

'You don't know what a workaholic you are. You will get bored in a day!'

'I do, but I also know how difficult it is to get someone you connect with so well. I have everything in life, and I am doing well at work. I have a comfortable life, maybe a life people dream about. But I want to be with Mihir. I am sure something or the other will work out for me there. I need to trust my abilities. This job cannot be the end of the world for me.'

'You are right. I remember the time when I was trying hard for a transfer to Kolkata just to be with Pranab. I can totally understand the dilemma. My situation was different because I was coming back to my people and I also didn't have to leave my job, but presented with a situation where I was to choose between my job and Pranab, there's no way I would have chosen my job. But you are leaving the country as well so things might be very different for you. Just remember that the road might get rocky and at that point, don't stop believing in yourself.'

'Thanks, Rhea. I will miss you at the wedding.'

The wedding was a private affair held in Dehradun. Neeti and Mihir wanted a quiet ceremony with only close relatives and friends. Mihir's parents and close friends, including Shishir, flew from Mumbai to Dehradun for the festivities.

'You've done us proud,' Neeti's aunt exclaimed with a beaming and most likely fake smile. Neeti tried to figure out what exactly she had done to do anyone proud. She was getting married. People fall in love, people get married, and she thought it was pretty normal. Then her aunt completed her sentence, 'You are going to America, you have done us so proud.' Now she understood: she was getting married to a guy who lived in the United States of America, and that was supposedly a thing to be proud of.

'Thank you, Aunty,' Neeti responded with an uncomfortable smile. She was still in disbelief that even in the year 2011, people had such thoughts. She would have married someone in India if she had connected with him and things had worked out. It just so happened that she fell in love with Mihir and they held on to each other and decided to get married. Going to the US was incidental, and also problematic to an extent because she would probably have to give up her stable career to be with the one she loved.

Moving to the US was not something Neeti had ever anticipated. Mumbai was her dreamland and she was content there, but destiny took a turn and she was not only leaving Mumbai but also the country she belonged to. Neeti was in conversation with her seniors at work and the members of her family regarding leaving her job. Everyone knew how important this job was to Neeti and how much effort it had taken her to get selected and then to rise up the ladder. Her family, friends, and colleagues suggested not to resign immediately and continue to be on a long leave and decide on it a couple of months later, after weighing all the pros and cons. Neeti also wanted to take some more time to decide, so she took a long leave rather than resigning right away.

Neeti looked beautiful in the wedding *lehenga* and could not stop staring at herself in the mirror. She was doing what her heart had desired and when you listen to your heart, it reflects on your face. She was glowing and her cheeks had turned crimson, matching the colour of her *lehenga*. She missed Rhea, who could not make it to the wedding because it was very close to her delivery date, but they did speak over the phone and Rhea could not have been happier; her best friend was finally getting married to the guy she was madly in love with.

'I feel like the luckiest guy in the world right now,' Mihir said as soon as he saw Neeti in her wedding *lehenga*.

'I can't wait to spend the rest of my life with you,' Neeti was beaming.

The day after the wedding, Neeti and Mihir took a flight from Delhi to Kansas City. Neeti started feeling sick mid-flight. She had high fever and was shivering. Mihir tried to cover her with multiple blankets, but nothing worked. When she collapsed standing in the immigration line, he grasped that it was something that couldn't wait, so he rushed her to the Kansas City Medical Center Emergency Room, and the moment the doctors saw her, they arranged to get her admitted. She got a serious infection that had reached her kidney. Any further delay could have meant endangering her life. Neeti was in intense pain but was still conscious.

'Are you employed?' the nurse asked. It was one of the several standard questions the staff asked before registering a patient in the hospital system.

'Not here, not in this country,' Neeti replied. Neeti was then taken to a private room and an intravenous drip was immediately administered. The doctors also ordered an array of tests and scans. This wasn't the greatest start to their married life, and to make matters worse, she couldn't let go of the question that the nurse asked her about her employment status. Neeti was in a hospital emergency room, with acute pain, but more than her pain she was worried about her employment status. To get married, have a home, and be a homemaker was one of the things she was eagerly looking forward to, but when the nurse asked her about her employment status, something hit her hard. She wanted to make it clear to the nurse that she was employed, only in a different country. Not sure why, but it struck her for the first time that being employed was a prominent part of one's identity. It is the first question everyone asks when they meet you, even in a hospital. People assess your success, your achievements, and even your worth, by your employment status. 'I'm fighting a life-threatening infection and the nurse was asking me about my employment status. How come I never gave this question any importance every time I went to the hospital for my yearly checkups?' she thought to herself.

Neeti was in the hospital for three days. The doctors and nurses kept a close watch on her heart rate and vitals. She was on intravenous drip the whole time and the medication made her drowsy and she slept most of the time. Mihir was constantly checking Neeti's temperature and kept holding her hand. For these three days, Mihir slept on a chair next to Neeti's bed. On the fourth day, she was discharged and given strict instructions to have plenty of fluids and get ample rest. She spent the next two days at home, resting and sleeping. Even though she had had a life-threatening infection, Neeti did not want to be treated as someone who was sick. She was a newly wedded bride and wanted to enjoy the post-marital bliss.

'How are you feeling now? Here's your medication. If you aren't feeling too tired, would you like to go out for a bit?' Mihir asked as he pulled a chair to sit next to the bed.

'I'm feeling much better now, and I also want to go out. I am actually bored lying in bed all the time,' Neeti said.

Mihir and Neeti went to the 36th Street where most of the restaurants were. It was closer to home and also the university.

'Let me take you to my favourite pizza place. I have spent many evenings here, working on my assignments. The owner and I have almost become friends now.'

'Okay, but I will only have iced tea. I don't really feel like eating anything.'

Mihir held Neeti's hand and went to place the order.

'Hey, buddy! How have you been? Long time! This beautiful lady must be Neeti,' the owner said excitedly.

'Hi, Steve! Yes, this is my beautiful wife, Neeti,' Mihir beamed proudly.

'Congratulations, Mihir!'

'Thank you.'

Mihir introduced Neeti to his friend, Steve and then they grabbed a table near the window as they waited for their order.

'How did he recognize me?' Neeti asked.

'I used to video chat with you from here. Also, most of my friends here know about you.'

'This is embarrassing and flattering at the same time.'

'Every time you would ask me if I was sure about you, I used to think that this girl doesn't know what she is talking about.'

Neeti met some of Mihir's close friends later on and was overwhelmed with the kind of warmth she received. She didn't feel like she was meeting them for the first time because Mihir had already told them a great deal about her; she felt like she was meeting her own friends back home. She was happy about her decision to marry him and move to the US. But the one thing that kept hovering in her head over and over again was—her employment status!

Although Neeti was still technically employed at that time, she was going to be a stay-at-home wife soon, if she decided to resign from her job. She was on a long leave and had to decide one way or the other shortly. The decision to quit the job wasn't an easy one to make. Neeti loved her work and excelled at it. But living in Mumbai alone after getting married was not a feasible option either. She had given a lot of thought to deciding on moving to the US, to leave her job, and to become a housewife, at least until the time she got her work authorization. She was almost certain about it when she had left India, but after her visit to the Emergency Room, she was getting second thoughts. All these doubts were unsettling. She knew that instead of brooding over it and not getting anywhere, she probably should seek guidance. Unsure if her decision was right, she picked up the phone and called her mentor, Shekhar.

'Hi, Shekhar. How are you doing? Is this a good time to talk?'

'Hi, Neeti. What a pleasant surprise! How are you doing? How is married life treating you?'

'I am doing well, thank you. I wanted to talk to you about something.'

'Sure, go ahead. You sound glum. Is everything all right?'

'Yes, everything is fine. I just am not too sure about my decision to quit my job. I was sure about it until the time I was in India, but certain things here have made me realize that I associate my identity with my work. Every time I think about quitting my job, I think about all the blood, sweat, and tears that went into reaching the position I am at now, and it will all be gone the moment I resign. I will be jobless, and will be left with literally no identity of my own.'

'You know something, Neeti? When you joined the organization, I knew you were different, in the way you conducted yourself, the way you interacted with your peers and seniors, and the way you fiercely put your points across, without any inhibitions. That was precisely the reason why I wanted you to work in the dematerialization scam investigation. Your sincerity and work ethic are incomparable.'

'Thanks, Shekhar, but this is making me feel that I am probably making the wrong decision.'

'Neeti, you underestimate yourself, but I have seen your work. You don't know what you are capable of, and I am here to let you know that you are immensely capable. You are at the threshold of your new life, a life that you and Mihir are going to create together, and it requires your attention. Your work life is only a part of your identity, it's not your whole identity. Also, what you have done will never go to waste. This experience will definitely help you in the future in ways you probably can't envisage right now. If you are thinking you are never going to work again, let me tell you—you are not that person. So, stop mulling over things and start enjoying your marital bliss. Go ahead and resign from the job. It's not the end of the world,' Shekhar talked for about half an hour and Neeti kept listening.

By the end of the call, she was ready to make the decision. She reckoned that there was no way she was going to continue working in Mumbai leaving Mihir in the US and therefore decided to resign from the job. She was required to resign in person and also needed to serve the notice period. So, she took the first available flight to Mumbai to finally tender her resignation.

'I can see the post-marital glow on your face,' Shekhar said.

'Thanks, Shekhar. I married the man I love and I am truly happy. Maybe that's what is getting reflected on my face,' Neeti replied.

'So, have you finally made up your mind?'

'Yes. I hope I am doing the right thing.'

'Where is my confident warrior? Why this self-doubt, Neeti?'

'It's probably the fear of the unknown.'

'You are doing the right thing, let go of your doubts.'

'Thanks, Shekhar. I will miss you, and I will miss this office.'

'We will miss you too, Neeti. But it's time to move on.'

Neeti returned to the US on a dependent visa. Mihir was still technically a student at that time, and being a dependent of a student, Neeti couldn't work or study. Mihir was on an F-1 visa and Neeti got her F-2 visa based on Mihir's. All she could do as a dependent of a student visa-holder was either volunteer with some organization or stay at home. But that did not dampen her spirits because at this point, she was excited about this new journey. She always had a tremendous regard for housewives and thought there was so much to do at home—cook, clean, turn your house into a home, and all those romantic thoughts associated with being a housewife when you never had imagined becoming one.

Mihir had been living in Kansas City for a considerable period of time and by now he knew the place inside out. In the initial few days, he showed Neeti around and introduced her to his friends, and then one day they went to attend a birthday party. The party was at a hall in an apartment complex that was specifically designated for events, get-togethers and parties. There was music, some space for dancing, and chairs for people who preferred to sit.

'Hi, my name is Amita. You can call me Amy. Are you a student here?' one of the girls at the party asked Neeti. Mihir had gone to help his friend with food and drinks for the party and therefore it looked like Neeti was by herself there.

'No, I got married recently and came here a couple of months ago.'

'Oh, shortcut!' Amy remarked, with a smug smile.

It took Neeti some time to process this remark. She was flabbergasted. 'What did this woman just say?' she wondered. Then she looked at her with eyes wide open as Amy got up to find herself a drink. Neeti was clueless as to what to say. She was new to the country and its people. Surprised by the unexpected remark, Neeti chose not to respond.

'Would you like to eat now?' Mihir came back and asked.

'Sure,' Neeti replied. Although she ate food, she was trying to digest the comment she had got from Amy. They came back home and Neeti was still thinking about Amy's comment. Words have the power to heal and a superpower to penetrate our hearts and hit the spot that hurts the most. 'I resigned from my job after much deliberation and this is the first time I am socializing after handing over my resignation. If this is the kind of reaction I am going to get from the people around, I will probably end up regretting my decision. I did not want to come to the US and surely did not want any shortcuts. I came to this country simply because my husband lives here. Why is it so difficult to understand!' she thought.

All this reminded her of the comment from her aunt who claimed to be proud that Neeti was going to the US after getting married. When she put the two comments together, she realized for the first time that coming to the US perhaps is a dream for many people and maybe some people consider getting married to someone who lives in the US, a shortcut to getting here. She was not aware of it and almost felt naïve that she was getting to know all this through personal experiences.

'While we all live in the same world, our mini-worlds comprise what we see, observe, and deal with on a day-to-day basis. It forms our perspective. Maybe the perspectives of these people were formed based on their experiences and observations,' she told herself, but her truth was far removed from these experiences of people, so she decided to take it all with a pinch of salt. 'I wish I had known this before, maybe I would have been better prepared mentally,' she mused. It was 3 a.m. and she was still wide awake.

'Neeti, why are you still up? Is everything all right?' Mihir woke up from his sleep and asked Neeti. She then told him everything that had happened at the party.

'Don't pay attention to these kind of people. They live in their bubbles and know nothing beyond their small worlds. Such trifling remarks from people who don't matter to us should not bother you, but if it's troubling you, we will not hang out with that group anymore. You don't need to lose sleep over all this. Please sleep now,' Mihir said as he gave her a kiss.

The next morning Neeti woke up and told herself that she would forget this incident, considering it as a bad dream and would not let it affect her. She told herself that she would explore the city, its people, and concentrate on her well-being. She decided to go to the university gym. It was a large gym with a plethora of workout equipment. She started with the treadmill. She had hardly spent a couple of minutes on it when a petite girl who was working out on the next treadmill greeted her with a warm smile. Neeti smiled back.

'Hi, I am Niharika. I have never seen you here before. Are you new to the city?' the girl asked.

'Yes, I came here a month ago. My husband recently got his PhD from here. I don't know anyone else here,' Neeti responded.

'Oh, we have a large community of Indians here. I will introduce you to everyone. We will make sure you never feel lonely,' Niharika said.

They chatted for some more time and then exchanged phone numbers. Niharika asked Neeti to meet her at the library the next day. Neeti came back home and shortly afterwards Mihir was home too.

'How was your day?' Neeti asked Mihir.

'Usual, was working on finishing up an experiment for my research paper. How was yours?'

'I made an acquaintance today. Her name is Niharika. I met her at the gym. She told me about an Indian community here.'

'I know that an Indian community exists but I've never been greatly involved with it so far, but if you are interested, I would join the community too.'

Neeti got up the next morning, and after finishing the chores, she packed her backpack and headed to the library. Niharika was waiting for her at the library with a couple of other people from the Indian community. Niharika introduced Neeti to everyone and they told Neeti that they were planning to meet in a couple of days for a birthday celebration and Mihir and Neeti should join in too.

Neeti and Mihir went for the birthday party and some more birthday celebrations thenceforth. Since Kansas City was a relatively smaller city, the Indian community was close-knit and they met one another pretty often. As days passed by, Neeti became more and more involved with the activities of the community. They would go to a different restaurant for each birthday celebration and this way Neeti got to explore the city as well.

One night, Neeti went with the group for a girls' night out. She was out and about without Mihir for the first time, although he called and texted her every hour or so. For the first time, she felt that she was getting a hang of the place, and that she had finally found a circle of her own.

It was almost time for Diwali. Neeti was now an active member of the group responsible for the arrangements for the Diwali celebration that their community had organized. She was also participating in a dance performance. The dance group met every night for rehearsals and also stayed up late. Everyone was burning the midnight oil to perfect the dance moves and the rehearsals were a great deal of fun. Late-night games and dinners with the group made Neeti feel connected to everyone.

'We will do the final rehearsals today at the auditorium. Make sure you get all your costumes,' the coordinator said.

'Neeti, my dress is a bit too loose. Please sew it up for me so that I can wear it tomorrow. We all have work or school to go to, and honestly, I don't even know how to sew. You are a housewife and must have ample amount of free time,' one of the girls said.

There was an awkward silence in the room. Neeti did not say anything. She wanted to scream and tell everyone that she had been working for more than seven years and became a housewife just a month ago. She was appalled by the attitude some people had towards housewives and how they saw them differently from someone who was working or studying, but she did not want to create a scene there. The girl was not happy with Neeti's silence and decided to get the dress sewed from a professional tailor. Neeti did not want this to affect her mood or her performance and decided not to pay too much attention to what others perceived of her or of housewives in general, focusing instead on the Diwali preparations. Finally, the D-day arrived. The event was a grand success and everyone was ecstatic.

'I didn't know you danced so well,' Mihir said.

'I didn't know you knew how to whistle,' Neeti replied.

'You could see me whistle from the stage?'

'I can never take my eyes off you.'

'You looked ravishing. I recorded the whole dance sequence on my phone.'

'Thanks,' Neeti said with a smile. She did not want to bring up what had happened the day before. She was glad that the performance went well and did not want to ruin her moments of happiness. Life wasn't bad except for those extremely hurtful comments from random strangers here and there. Neeti was cheerful most of the time and also busy with events, potlucks, and birthday parties. However, she still felt unaccomplished, for obvious reasons—success to her meant getting adulation at work. A clean house, a cozy home, well-prepared meals, social gatherings, and dance performances did not make the cut. Because she felt unaccomplished, the random comments from people around started making a dent on her self-esteem.

The days were getting colder and Neeti was home one day and didn't feel like going out. Her phone rang. It was her mom.

'Hi, Maa. How are you doing?'

'I'm doing well. I saw the pics and videos of Diwali celebrations that you posted on Facebook. You look gorgeous. That dance performance was absolutely splendid!'

'Thanks, Maa.'

'What's wrong? Why do you sound like this?'

'I'm just feeling low because of the weather. You know that I don't like winter, and it's getting awfully cold here. The snowstorms are making life really difficult.'

'Are you sure it's the weather?'

'Yeah, and I am also getting bored sitting at home, the life of a housewife isn't something I am used to. Also, people around me are making things even more difficult for me.'

'Did anyone say something?'

'Nothing in particular, just general remarks about housewives that I had never heard before. People are too presumptuous and say hurtful things without knowing anything about you or your situation.'

'Since when have you started getting bothered about what people have to say?'

'I don't know why and how all this has started affecting me. I was never this person.'

'You need to relax a little bit and learn to enjoy life and try not to get affected by what others have to say. You are in a new place with unfamiliar surroundings and unknown people, give yourself some time to adjust to all this.'

Neeti took her mom's advice seriously and decided not to let others' opinions affect her and resolved to focus on her life and her household.

'I think I should start volunteering,' Neeti told Mihir one night after he was back from work. 'All the fun things are great and I am having a good time here, but I need to do something more productive with my time. My empty mind is becoming a devil's workshop. I am thinking of volunteering at the Kansas City Medical Center. I would love to help the health system assist its patients,' she continued.

'I am finishing up assignments in my current lab and am applying for post-doctoral fellowships all over the country. We will move out of Kansas City soon, but if you want to volunteer, please do. It's up to you what you want to do with your time. I didn't suggest it because I thought you have been working for a long time and a little break won't hurt. But if it's not what you want, you can go check out the volunteering positions available at the medical centre,' Mihir said.

Neeti visited the website of the Kansas City Medical Center and looked for volunteering positions and applied for a few of them. In a couple of days, she was called for an interview and was also selected for a volunteering position. She started volunteering a week later, after taking the Health Insurance Portability and Accountability Act (HIPAA) course, getting the immunizations, and clearing all the background checks. The work involved helping patients navigate the hospital, and at times she would escort the patients to the right place they needed to be. The hospital had recently moved to a new building and the patients and their families were finding it difficult to locate the departments and wards within the hospital. Neeti found this job to be particularly fulfilling. She was not getting paid for the work she was doing, but she was content. She was happy that she could find something meaningful to do. Many people get paid but don't like their jobs; Neeti liked what she did and there was little to complain about.

She would wake up every morning and pack her breakfast. She didn't pack lunch because she liked eating in the cafeteria with Mihir, as he worked in the same campus. She walked to the medical centre from home and it was a short and pleasant walk. Kansas City was not very crowded and people smiled at each other when they saw you in the streets. Neeti loved these walks in the morning. After reaching the medical centre, she would sit in the reception area and ask the patients if they needed any help. Watching the patients, Neeti also realized the frailty of life. There were patients of all ages, races, and sexuality. Some days she would see little kids with terminal illnesses and would cry after coming back home, on other days she would celebrate someone's battle over deadly diseases.

Although there was designated staff to carry people on wheelchairs, Neeti did not hesitate to give a helping hand when required. She worked with the Securities Market Regulator in India until a couple of months ago, and now she was carrying people on wheelchairs without even getting paid for it. That was quite a drastic change in her work profile, but she was gratified.

She knew that at both the places she was helping people live a better life. While the thought that she left a secure job and not being eligible to work did cross her mind occasionally, she did not let that take away the joy she was deriving from what she was doing at present.

It was a regular day for Neeti. She went to the medical centre and started working. She was sitting at the front desk when one of Mihir's colleagues stopped by. She started sweating and a feeling of inferiority complex began to creep over her. She did not make eye contact with her and pretended to search for something in the drawer while another volunteer helped her. That was the first time Neeti felt that she was probably trying to suppress a feeling that had started growing inside her mind like a weed. She felt ashamed of the fact that she was not eligible to work and she was doing something that was not in line with her education and training. This thought was slowly creeping into her head and she wanted to address it immediately.

'Mihir, I am very happy doing what I am doing, but I think I am capable of doing so much more. Is there a way I can start working? Something more in line with my credentials?'

'On this visa, I am afraid volunteering is what you can do, and I think about it at times and feel bad that you could do so much more but have to settle for this. Continue volunteering for some more time and once I get a post-doctoral fellowship, I might get a different visa, something like the J-visa, and you probably can start working then. I can't say for sure right now because all these discussions take place once you are selected for the position,' Mihir explained.

'Another option is to try and get a work visa, which honestly, at this point is almost like an unattainable dream. I probably should think about studying further, instead, but higher education in this country is pretty expensive, and being on a visa, I am not even eligible for any federal funding. Nevertheless, I can at least start studying for the entrance test, and I can keep the scores and apply to schools when we have the means to afford my education.'

'It's not a bad idea. That would also keep you occupied with something constructive.'

Mihir was applying to various universities for post-doctoral fellowships but was not entirely sure if that was going to change Neeti's work authorization situation. He was hoping to get a J-visa, and as a dependent of a J-visa holder, Neeti would be eligible to work. But there was also a possibility that he would be on Optional Practical Training (OPT) for another two years, and Neeti being his dependent would not be eligible to work for those two years. He had his fingers crossed and earnestly wished to get a J-visa for his post-doctoral fellowship.

Mihir finally got called to an interview for a post-doctoral fellow position from a health system in Baltimore. He and Neeti visited Baltimore, where they spent the entire day in the department of cell biology of the health system and went for dinner with the team later that evening. The team was cordial and made sure Neeti did not feel out of place and included her in conversations that weren't strictly related to work. She was not a science graduate and therefore everyone kept the topics of discussion generic so that there was no awkwardness.

'So, Neeti, what are your plans once Mihir and you move to Baltimore?' Mihir's potential supervisor asked.

'I will enroll in a law school,' Neeti promptly replied.

5

Life in the US

Mihir and Neeti returned to Kansas City from Baltimore after the interview and got back to their routine. Mihir was trying to finish his assignments in his current lab, while Neeti continued with her volunteering.

'Hi, are we meeting at the cafeteria for lunch now?' Neeti asked Mihir over the phone. It was usual for Neeti to call Mihir around lunchtime. They would then meet at the cafeteria and have lunch together.

'No, meet me at the chapel,' Mihir replied.

Neeti wondered why Mihir had changed the venue. She picked up her bag and headed towards the chapel, which was in the campus itself. Mihir had been going to the chapel regularly since he started pursuing his PhD. She reached the chapel and Mihir was standing at the aisle, with an envelope in his hand.

'I got selected for the fellowship,' Mihir said, hugging her.

'Oh, my God! Congratulations! And I was so worried as to why we were meeting in the chapel!' Neeti said with a sigh of relief. They both said a little prayer of thanks together.

'We need to start preparing for the move. I need to join on November 1st,' Mihir said.

'We still have some time. It's only the beginning of October, and we have a lot of friends here who can help us with the move,' Neeti assured Mihir. 'We don't know anyone in Baltimore though. Let me find out if there is any Indian community in Baltimore, like the one we have here. We can ask them about what living in Baltimore will be like. They can probably apprise us of the places to live there. I will also start doing some research online and learn more about the city,' she continued.

'I will also ask my prospective colleagues to help us familiarize with the place.'

'Talking about the Indian community, I think we should call them over for dinner before leaving the city.'

'It's a good idea. Do you want to order pizzas?'

'I think I should cook for them. I don't know if we will meet them ever again.'

'All right, I will help you with the preparations.'

Neeti and Mihir called their friends over and they made sure they prepared enough food for the entire group. Mihir took the day off because he needed to run errands not only for dinner but also for preparations for their move to Baltimore. Almost everyone from the Indian community showed up in the evening. Mihir and Neeti were glad that they were able to meet them all one last time before leaving.

'You are lucky, Mihir,' one of the guys in the group said.

'Thanks,' Mihir replied with a smile.

'It's a blessing to have a wife who stays home and cooks delicious food for you every day,' the guy continued. Mihir looked at Neeti and gestured her to ignore the innuendo. After everyone left, Mihir talked to Neeti.

'Don't feel bad about these casual remarks. Our society has been conditioned to think a certain way for such a long time that it will take an equal amount of time to break these notions that people have about housewives. Some of these things are ingrained in people's minds. They probably don't even think these things through before spurting them out. Moreover, some of these people know nothing about your background. I never used to hang out with them before you came here, so they know little about you. He was not a part of the subgroup you spent your time with while you were here, so he didn't even interact with you. He was just a random guy in the group, and his remark doesn't mean anything. We are moving to another place, let's leave the bad memories here and focus on what's in store for us,' Mihir reasoned.

'I understand that. But these comments are hurtful. I know he didn't mean any harm but I wish there were a way to change people's mindsets about housewives. But I'm too tired to think about all this right now and we need to prepare for the move too. Let's go to sleep,' Neeti said.

Neeti and Mihir started packing their belongings and their friends came to help them on the day of the move. With everything packed in the trailer attached to their car, Neeti and Mihir began their road trip to Baltimore. They were not entirely sure about how life would be in Baltimore but they were excited about the next phase of their life and hoped it would be a good one. Neeti had spent only six months in Kansas City but had got attached to the place because of the treatment and warmth she received from most people. There were some bumps along the way, but by and large people were friendly and made Neeti feel at ease during the very first few days of her stay in the US. She tried contacting some Indian communities but managed to get only a lukewarm response. Finally, one guy responded and that gave Neeti a ray of hope. She asked some questions about Baltimore and he gave generic responses, which wasn't of much help. Therefore, Neeti and Mihir decided to trust their internet research on the basic information they needed to set foot in the city.

It took them almost three days to reach Baltimore. They made sure they took enough breaks on the way to enjoy their road trip, and finally, they were in Charm City.

'When you met me at Prithvi Café, you wouldn't have imagined a life like this, I'm sure. I'm sorry my life goals are making you move around so much.'

'You don't have to be sorry. I am glad that I am getting exposed to a different kind of life, a different culture, and most importantly, I'm getting to do all this with you.'

'All of this will make sense, eventually. I promise.'

'I trust you. Now get out of the car, we need to check-in at the guest house!'

They stayed in a guest house for the first few days. It was a row house that had been turned into a guest house by the owners. This was the first time Neeti was seeing row houses. Space was definitely at a premium in Baltimore, she thought. Baltimore and Kansas City were strikingly different. Baltimore had a long and rich history, so the buildings were old and had historical relevance. It was teeming with people and was demographically different from Kansas City. Neeti was pleased to see the diversity, but was also beleaguered with the fear of the unknown. There were stark differences between the two cities: Kansas City was calm, while Baltimore was hustling and bustling; the sparsely populated streets of Kansas City were clean and quiet whereas the streets of Baltimore were crowded and busy; the laid-back life of Kansas City was in direct contrast with Baltimore that seemed to be on the run all day long.

While Mihir had to immediately report to work the morning after they reached Baltimore, Neeti remained in the guest house alone. She made herself a cup of coffee and sat on the couch as she pondered over how she would be able to manage alone at home in a fast-paced city like Baltimore with no close-knit Indian community. Mihir called to let her know that he wouldn't be back for lunch as his lab had arranged for a welcome lunch for him, and Neeti remained in the guest house by herself the whole day. She went downstairs and watched TV. Mihir came back in the evening, and Neeti described her first day to him. Mihir described his and he was excited about the prospects that awaited him in this new lab.

'This lab will definitely help me with my research goals. I would be working on drosophila and I can't explain how excited I am to get started. I just feel bad that you are stuck in this guest house. I am pretty sure you will feel a lot better once we move into an apartment,' assured Mihir.

'Did they tell you anything about your visa category?' Neeti asked.

'I will be on Optional Practical Training (OPT). I asked them if I could be on any other visa category where a dependent spouse could work at this point and they said no to that.'

'That means I cannot work for another two years,' Neeti was crestfallen.

'Let me get settled in the lab. I will ask around if there are any other options available. Please don't feel dejected. All of the things that I am achieving right now would mean nothing if it would not make you happy. I am doing everything to make sure we have a beautiful life together. Just hang in there for some more time.'

Student visa holders under science, technology, engineering, and mathematics (STEM) degrees get an OPT for a year and an extension for another year. Since Mihir's PhD qualified under STEM, he was to be on OPT for two years.

The news put cold water on Neeti's hopes to work in the immediate future. She was heartbroken but did not want to react because it was the start of Mihir's journey as a post-doctoral fellow. She wanted to be a support rather than a hurdle in his professional pursuits.

The next day was the same story, but Neeti was mentally prepared for it, so it did not feel as terrible as the first day. Her mind was besieged with thoughts though, mostly negative. She told herself that she would deal with one problem at a time. Right now the most important thing for them was to look for a place to live in.

'Can we please start looking for an apartment? I think being in the guest house all day long perhaps is the reason why I am getting this anxiety,' Neeti told Mihir. He agreed, and they started house hunting immediately. In Baltimore, the apartment complexes were huge, unlike in Kansas City. They looked like hotel rooms when you entered the complex, and most of them felt like hotel rooms even on the inside. Neeti did not feel any connection with the humongous concrete buildings. Adding to this, Baltimore had an atrocious rodent situation and Neeti was unequivocally clear that she was not going to step her foot in an apartment whose management wouldn't give an assurance that there would be no rodents in the apartment.

'You are a lab rat. I don't want to deal with any other rats at home, please,' Neeti said jokingly.

'Don't worry, I am equally averse to having any kind of rodents at home. My love for them is only limited to the lab,' Mihir replied.

They kept searching and kept getting disappointed every single time. No management was ready to give assurance regarding the rodent situation. One week passed by and Neeti was now getting desperate. She crossed her fingers for this last apartment complex that they were about to visit.

'Let's look at this apartment complex, and if you don't like this one as well, we will have to finalize an apartment from the ones we have seen so far. If you are looking for an apartment complex like the one we had in Kansas City, you probably will only get disappointed,' Mihir told Neeti.

This apartment complex was in the heart of the city but was surprisingly insulated from the noise and clutter. It had a large backyard, which was still green as it had not started snowing yet. The front driveway was covered with trees, most of them had shed leaves, but you could imagine how it would look in spring with trees on either side. They visited an apartment on the second floor, for some reason it did not have an apartment-like feel to it, and it definitely didn't feel like a hotel room as was the case with the others. It felt like a standalone house. The flooring was wooden and the walls were off-white. The living room was spacious and had three large windows overlooking the trees in the backyard of the apartment complex. The dining area was attached to the living room, and the kitchen was right next to it. A gallery from the living room led you to the bedroom which had a walk-in closet. You could access the bathroom from the bedroom as well as from the living room. The management had recently got the apartment cleaned and painted, you could smell the fresh paint. Neeti fell in love with the apartment instantly. The management assured that they were extremely proactive and diligent about pest control and there had been no complaints about rodents from any of the apartments under the management so far.

'I have found my home!' Neeti exclaimed.

Mihir hugged Neeti and finally they were relieved. They moved in and Neeti got busy turning the apartment into a home. She did some craftwork and a couple of paintings for their home. She would dust everything every day and would make sure to keep things in order. She was in love with her new home.

The home was set and Neeti now had a lot of time on her hands. She tried making friends in Baltimore, but everything here was different from how things were in Kansas City. People seemed busier and also kept to themselves most of the time. But eventually, she was able to make a few friends. The Indian community in Baltimore was not close-knit like it was in Kansas City. There were smaller and scattered groups unlike one large community in Kansas City. She reached out to one of the groups and they turned out to be warm and cordial. Neeti and Mihir started mingling with this group and began attending birthday parties, potlucks, Indian festivals, and other celebrations. People that were a part of this group lived in different areas in the city and therefore the group did not get together as often as was the case in Kansas City. Neeti was gradually coming to terms with the fact that Baltimore was less social as compared to Kansas City. She also realized that she was not the most extroverted person in the world and therefore making friends for her would be difficult if people weren't forthcoming. But she was slowly getting accustomed to the tepid social life that she would probably be having as long as they were in Baltimore.

Not that Neeti was too bothered about her social life, what disconcerted her the most was that she spent all her time at home without being productive. Even though she did household chores every day, she did not feel accomplished in the slightest degree. She thought about it every day and reckoned that perhaps she needed to change her mindset, maybe she needed to consider household work to be as significant as working professionally, but her mental block was too strong to break. To add to her woes, it started snowing. Everyone was expecting a white Christmas that winter. Homes, trees, cars—a thick layer of snow blanketed everything. Neeti never liked winters but when she glanced outside, it looked like a dream and was too beautiful to miss. She took a walk outside, clicked some pictures, and came back and made herself some ginger tea. This stroll gave her a respite from her unrelenting thoughts. She was exhausted from constantly thinking about being a housewife, not having work authorization, being alone at home all day, and feeling like she was not doing anything substantial in life.

Neeti started to contemplate why household work never qualifies as work per societal norms. So many women work at home every day without taking any days off for mild sickness, tiredness, or just because they need a break. They work 24/7 and are called housewives—someone who is not a professional, who doesn't bring in the moolah. They don't get paid, and their work is for the most part taken for granted. It's not that Neeti did not like doing household work, but even after spending the whole day working, at the end of the day she never felt that she had done anything worthwhile, and deep down this began troubling her.

Neeti called Rhea. She was the only one she could think of with whom she could have a heart-to-heart conversation.

'How are you doing?' Neeti asked Rhea.

'Doing pretty well. Work, home, family, keeps me on my toes and it's much more than I can handle. I think I need a break. How are you doing? All settled in Baltimore?'

'Baltimore is different from Kansas City, so I am still trying to get the hang of it. But I am not sure if I am still used to this life.'

'Used to what life?'

'The life of a housewife. I think it's got more to do with my mindset than anything else. I have never been a housewife before, so it's an alien feeling for me, and getting accustomed to it is becoming a challenge every single day.'

'To be honest, someone who was a workaholic like you, it's very hard for me to even imagine you being a housewife. I'm joking that I am tired of being this busy, but trust me I will feel so lost if I didn't have things to do that I am doing right now. You have survived more than six months without a job, that's commendable. Any updates on the work authorization part?'

'Right now I am on a dependent visa, that too dependent of a student. Mihir would be in the current status for at least the next two years, that means that I cannot work for the next two years under my current visa status. Even if he gets his H-1B visa after that, I still won't be eligible to work as his dependent. I would be able to work only if he gets a J-visa at the end of these two years. I should have probably researched a little more about life here. It's very different being home here than how it is back in India. Here, I hardly know my neighbours. At times I spend the entire day without seeing another human being until Mihir is back from the lab. Volunteering is my only option as of now, but my hands are tied even with respect to the kind of things I can volunteer for because of strict restrictions and guidelines around volunteering here. I don't see a light at the end of this tunnel that I probably have dug for myself.'

'Don't talk like this, things will get better.'

'I want to get out and work.'

'Why don't you try to distract yourself and go out and make some friends?'

'I know I am sounding like a broken record, but really, things are very different out here. There is very little interaction with the outside world, barring some social events like birthday parties, potlucks, and Indian festivals but I'm trying my best to reach out to people and make friends with them. I also miss the professional interactions. Working professionally is not just about working, it's also about having cerebral discussions and engaging conversations with your colleagues. Also, the whole jingbang of it, the projects, the deadlines, the presentations, and the happy hours! Now, it's a diametrically opposite situation for me and I am finding it difficult to cope with it. I'm not entirely regretting my decision to move to the US, but I'm definitely feeling desperate to go out and work.'

'I can totally understand what you are saying, but for now you have to keep the faith, distract yourself, and think about all the options you have. You aren't the one to break this easily. Where is the Neeti that came from a small town and made it big in the Maximum City?'

'I don't know Rhea. I think I am losing my identity. I am trying hard to keep it all together, but I'm not sure how long I can go on like this. Every day, I try to cook a new dish, do craftwork, or try to paint, but nothing is helping me get rid of these thoughts. Mihir tries to help by encouraging me to go out, mingle with people, join a book club, but I know that it's more of an internal battle than an external one and I need to fight it on my own. From being such a busy professional to leading a dreary life inside the four walls of an apartment is not easy to come to terms with.'

'Don't feel so low. Call me whenever you feel lonely, okay? I don't know much about the options you have, but all I can say is that I am there for you and you can call me anytime.'

'Thanks, Rhea.'

Neeti knew some women who had come to the US from India and who were in a similar situation as she was, with no work authorization, and she tried asking them how they coped with it. The response she got was that the thought of feeling unaccomplished did cross their minds, but they were so busy with their lives, household chores, and some with kids, that they really could not spend their energies brooding over lack of work authorization. When their visa categories would change, they would apply for employment authorization, because that's the most they could do and dwelling any more on that was futile. The ease with which everyone had accepted their destinies made Neeti uncomfortable and, in some corner of her mind, she started questioning if her restlessness was warranted.

One evening Neeti went for a walk with Pragya Maheshwari, one of the women from the Indian community who also had come to the US after getting married and just like her, didn't have work authorization.

'You seem impervious to your visa situation. Does it not bother you that you are not allowed to work here?' Neeti asked.

'What makes you think it doesn't bother me?' Pragya countered.

'You appear so calm, that's why.'

'Being restless about something you have little control over gets you nowhere. You will spoil your peace of mind and gain nothing by constantly thinking about it.'

'I agree, maybe I should stop being so restless, but there must be something we can do about our situation. I mean, we can get our work authorization, I believe. I'm alluding to getting a work visa.'

'You have no idea how difficult it is to get a work visa. Honestly, if you are too distressed about your situation, it doesn't hurt to try it out. Maybe we can get some inspiration from you and follow in your footsteps. At this point, I am not sure if I want to get into the struggle of getting my work authorization.'

'But how do you not feel that your education and experience need to be utilized. I know you used to work in India. Then how did you make peace with being a housewife after moving here?'

'I also had similar questions in my mind in the initial few months, but then I realized the travails of trying to get your work authorization and I gave up eventually.'

'Did you try applying for any jobs here?'

'Yes, at some places I could not proceed with my application beyond the point where they asked me whether I would need sponsorship, if the answer to the question was yes, I was not allowed to even go to the next step in the application process, which immediately put a damper on my plans to work here, and at places where I could proceed beyond that point, I did not get a response from them. People who come here to study find it easier to get a job. Do you have any plans or intentions to get higher education?'

'I do, but I am not eligible for any federal funding, but I can at least start thinking in that direction.'

Neeti came back home and Mihir was home too after a while.

'Hey, how was your day?' Mihir asked.

'I met Pragya and we had the same discussion regarding work authorization and visa. She told me that getting your work visa is a herculean task, she couldn't get it even after trying hard for it.'

'I think you need a break from these thoughts. You have your whole life to work, and you could have enjoyed this little break. But knowing the person you are, I know you would continue to feel restless unless you have something to do that is intellectually stimulating. Why don't you start preparing for your Law School Admission Test (LSAT)?'

'I guess you are right, I am pretty tired of these discussions. I need something constructive to occupy my mind.'

Neeti started preparing for her LSAT. The thought of going to a law school was not a random one. She felt that to get a job in the US, she would probably need some formal education from this country. With her experience at the Securities Market Regulator in India and as a company secretary, she had a solid background in corporate and securities law. She wanted to utilize her training and experience. She carefully weighed all the options between going for a master's degree, a business school, and a law school, and concluded that only law school could do justice to her qualification and experience.

Getting a law degree was expensive, Neeti and Mihir still did not have money to pay for law school. But Neeti wanted to take the LSAT and keep the scores in case something miraculously worked out and she was able to apply to a law school. Also, she needed a respite from the constant contemplation about her work situation and wanted to direct her energies into something intellectually stimulating. She ordered some books online and also got to know that their local library had some of the best books available for LSAT preparation. Every morning, she would get ready, have breakfast, put on her jacket and winter boots, and walk to the library that was about a mile from her house. Not that it was too much of a distance, but the cold was unforgiving. But she did not want the cold to be an excuse because again being home meant dealing with all those negative thoughts. She needed to get out and distract her mind with something stimulating.

She had a favourite spot at the library and would study there for hours. She would pack lunch with her and would have a break in between her study sessions and have her lunch. Mihir would meet her at the library every evening on his way back from his lab and they would come back home together. Some days it would get too cold, so she would wear an extra layer, but she knew how important it was for her to get out and get to the library to study. Neeti knew that consistency was the most important ingredient for success and took her preparation seriously and didn't miss a single day. She made sure to cook enough on the weekends so that she didn't have to cook every day. Mihir, as always, helped her with the chores so that she was able to concentrate more towards preparing for her exam.

Neeti liked going to the library because it filled her with positivity. She felt motivated to study because everyone else around would study sincerely too. Keeping herself motivated when she was alone at home was difficult, so she was glad she was doing this. She also made friends with a little girl who came to the library with her mother in the afternoon. She would wait for her every day and it was her favourite part of the day watching her play, learn, and listen to stories from her mom.

In a month, Neeti had finished working on all the problems from the book she had bought and also the one she was studying from at the library. Neeti ordered practice sets and attempted all the tests with utmost sincerity, using a timer and simulating exam-like conditions. She did not take any breaks in between and took the tests in one go like she would in a real exam. She was getting good scores, but she knew she could do better. She joined an online forum where people discussed the details of the test, what the test was like, how to prepare oneself for the test, and general questions relating to the test. The four-hour-long LSAT was also a test of your patience and temperament, not just reasoning, capability, and intelligence.

Finally, it was the day before the test. Mihir and Neeti visited the test venue to make sure they didn't end up wasting time looking for the exact location the next day.

'I'm really nervous. It's a four-hour-long test and I don't remember the last time I took one,' Neeti said.

'Don't be nervous. I have absolutely no doubt that you will totally rock it!'

'You overestimate me.'

'And you underestimate yourself.'

They woke up at 6 a.m. Mihir packed snacks for Neeti and made coffee for her. She shook nervously and Mihir held her hand during the drive to the test venue.

'Good luck,' Mihir said as he kissed Neeti on the forehead.

'Thanks. I need to run to the examination hall. I don't want to get late,' Neeti said as she rushed inside the double doors leading to the examination hall. Mihir went to a nearby coffee shop and waited there until the test was over.

'Oh, no. I can't even discuss the questions on the online forum. I am so anxious to know if I did them correctly,' Neeti said with a sigh as they celebrated the end of a gruelling and protracted test with an ice cream sundae. She was starving as she did not get time to have the snack that Mihir had packed for her.

Later, Neeti checked the online status every day, even twice a day to make sure if anyone was discussing their scores. Her anxiety levels were intensifying. After three weeks, she got an email with her test score. It was a decent score and gave Neeti some hopes about going to a law school.

'Congratulations!' Mihir said when he returned home that day.

'Thanks, but we can't afford the tuition right now. Would you like to attend the open house at the law school? That would help us get some more information about what our options are.'

'Sure.'

They attended the open house at the law school she wanted to apply to and looked at the information on federal funding. The only way she could go to school was if she had enough money to pay for it out of her pocket, which at this time was impossible. Neeti contacted the Office of Student Affairs of her preferred school, and they also suggested that she would have to either arrange funds from private lenders or pay it out of pocket. Given her situation, Neeti would not be eligible for any federal funding, and private funding was available not only at a high interest rate, but also required her to provide a guarantor. She hardly knew anyone in the US, and therefore did not feel comfortable approaching someone to act as a guarantor.

Despite a decent LSAT score, without funding, it was not possible for Neeti to apply to the school. She was not entirely sure how she was going to fund her education. Even after having worked extremely hard to get to this point, there was no way for her to overcome this hurdle at the moment. There was absolutely no point sulking about it, so she decided to put her dreams in the parking lot for now and do something productive with her time.

She went online and started researching her options. She almost felt like she was back to square one. As someone on a dependent visa, she was only eligible to volunteer. So, she started searching for places where she could make use of her experience and skillsets. As a volunteer, you are not eligible to do any job which could possibly mean taking the job of a paid worker, so her options were limited to only the places that did offer volunteering positions. She applied to a health system that had a volunteering services office and started coordinating with them over email.

6

What Next!

A few days had passed since Neeti had applied for the volunteering position, and she had not heard from the office yet. Sitting on her couch, she was constantly looking for notifications on her phone. She kept refreshing her inbox over and over again in the hope of getting that one email until she resigned to the fact that probably today wasn't the day. Baltimore was a bigger city than Kansas City and so was the health system she had applied to for the volunteering position. Therefore, the processing of the application would have a longer waiting period, as compared to the health system she was volunteering for in Kansas City, she thought. She tried her best to spend the next few days cooking, cleaning, and doing household chores. She also tried her hands at some DIY projects. But all she had at the back of her mind was the volunteering position she had applied for. Then, finally one morning the phone rang. It was a call from the volunteering services office of the health system she had applied to. They had called to schedule a meeting with Neeti.

Neeti was relieved that at least an appointment was now scheduled. She was finally able to see some light at the end of the dark tunnel she had been walking through for many months. On the day of the appointment, she dressed up in a skirt suit and showed up on time. Mihir accompanied her. The Volunteering Services Manager was delighted to see Neeti being interested in volunteering. She was asked to take the HIPAA test and complete all the paperwork. Neeti submitted the paperwork and the manager looked at Neeti's address.

'Neeti, how do you plan to commute to the office?' the manager asked.

'I will take the Health System shuttle.'

'You live pretty far from here. There is no direct shuttle to this office from where you live. You probably will have to take a shuttle to the main campus, then another one from the main campus to this, which will take you about an hour and a half,' the manager said.

'Oh, I didn't realize that,' Neeti was disappointed and anxious that she might lose this opportunity. 'I don't mind taking two shuttles, it's completely fine,' Neeti responded.

'You don't have to do that. We have another office, a stone's throw from your place. Let me connect you with the people over there, but you will have to give an interview as they are very specific about the kind of people they hire, even for volunteering positions,' the manager said.

'Sure.'

The Volunteering Services Manager connected Neeti with the manager at the other office and Neeti was scheduled for an interview. For this interview, she wore a pair of navy-blue trousers and a light blue shirt with white stripes. She tied her hair neatly in a ponytail and wore light makeup. She looked sharp. Mihir came home early to provide her moral support.

He dropped her at the office and asked her to give him a call once the interview was over. He drove back home, opened the main door, and sat on the couch to watch something on TV as he waited for Neeti to get done with the interview. As soon as he sat down, his phone rang.

'I am done,' Neeti said. Mihir was confused, he had dropped Neeti off at the office only five minutes back and she was now done. He drove back to the office and asked Neeti what had happened.

'They loved me,' Neeti was exhilarated. 'I will join as soon as the background checks and other formalities are complete,' Neeti was beaming. She was thrilled that she would be able to be productive. The fact that she was productive at home did not count one bit. She wanted a 'real' job, even if it was unpaid.

Neeti started volunteering the following week. She liked the work environment and also made some friends in the office. She reported to work on time and was sincere towards every task assigned to her. One day around lunchtime, she noticed a line outside the office cafeteria and wondered what it was all about.

'Neeti, today is World Environment Day, and the office is giving away some plants. Let's go and get ours,' Aarti, Neeti's colleague, said excitedly. Aarti was one of the friends Neeti had made at work. Although she hardly had any time to socialize, there were a couple of people in the office she liked to interact with if she had any spare time during breaks. Aarti worked in a different department at the same company. They would meet over lunch or coffee sometimes, given that life was busy for both. Aarti was ambitious and worked full-time and was also pursuing a master's degree in order to get better work opportunities. She was nursing a baby but that did not deter from pursuing her professional goals.

'No, you go. I am just a volunteer, the plants are for the employees,' Neeti replied feeling unsure. This thought kept troubling her every day that she was a volunteer and not an employee.

'Come on, the office does not discriminate between who is an employee and who isn't, and you come here and work, so that makes you eligible for the gift.'

'For some reason, I don't feel comfortable.'

'You need to broaden your mindset. I was also in your situation once, and I can totally relate to what you are going through, but now I have my work visa. You will get there and don't get bogged down by what life has thrown at you.'

Neeti smiled and went with Aarti and got a parsley plant which she placed in her kitchen after getting back home that evening.

'I got a parsley plant from the office. It's a gift,' Neeti told Mihir with a broad smile. Mihir had not seen Neeti this happy in a long time. He understood where her happiness came from. She wanted to work professionally and needed a sense of belonging with the organization she was working with. This volunteering opportunity was a perfect fit for her. She carried out her responsibilities as a volunteer earnestly. Although it was not a paid position, she valued it immensely because it provided her something to look forward to every morning. She was appreciative of the professional interactions and learnt something new every day. Moreover, she was delighted to get exposure to a different work culture and was positive that it would help her in the long run.

Neeti had learned to make some quick lunches as she did not want to spend money on lunch when she was not earning anything. Lemon rice was her favourite as it was easy to make and needed very little prep time. Most of her colleagues brought lunch too, so it was a good way to have some social interaction during lunchtime. The days were packed with work and a lot of learning, and Neeti would come home reasonably tired. Mihir would then make a cup of tea for her and they would take turns to prepare dinner.

'Neeti, it has been almost two months since you have been volunteering with us. Would you like to gain some experience regarding how the purchasing decisions are made with the vendors?' Neeti's supervisor asked.

'Sure, this is something I would love to be a part of. It will be a great learning experience for me,' Neeti said.

She then spent that morning learning the nuances of how purchasing decisions are made at a health system. The deal involved millions of dollars and Neeti realized what a massive health system it was. She was content with her life, but she always wondered how much different it would be if only she had work authorization. She could have participated in the purchasing negotiations and decision-making. Being a volunteer, her hands were tied. She was learning substantially, but she also wanted to contribute towards the things that mattered and, as of now, she wasn't legally allowed to do those things, despite being capable and willing.

Neeti had been volunteering for the last three months and the team had accepted her like their very own. She was pleasantly surprised that even though she was from another country and culture, and had an accent different from everyone else, her colleagues never made her feel that she didn't belong there. People in her office were welcoming and encouraging. Whenever she wanted to learn something new or wanted to take a lead on something, no one pulled her down because she was just a volunteer. She was included in the office celebrations, events, and functions and was treated the same way the other employees were treated. Neeti was apprehensive of Baltimore during the initial few days, but now she was thankful that they had moved to a place that was so warm and welcoming. She had started connecting with the city the same way she had connected with Mumbai. She was regular at work and was becoming a familiar face in the office. The office building had several other departments and people from those departments also started noticing Neeti.

'Hey, there is an open position in your department. Would you like to apply for it? Someone from your department told me about it in the break room,' Aarti asked Neeti.

'I would love to,' Neeti said excitedly.

'You are already in the system, so applying for the job through the intranet would not take long. I will send you the link to the position. Just keep your resumé ready and apply for the position as soon as you can.'

'You are really kind. I appreciate all that you do for me.'

'I see a lot of me in you. I also came to the US after getting married, and I can never forget all the days when I was clueless about what to do in a place where I didn't know anyone except my husband. I also started as a volunteer and it makes my heart full every time I see someone tread the same path as me. It makes me feel that there is a ray of hope for every woman who comes to this country leaving her family and career behind.'

Aarti's words felt like a warm hug to Neeti and she was almost lachrymose. What she had just said was in stark contrast with the harsh reactions and remarks about housewives that Neeti had received from some people in Kansas City. Aarti made Neeti feel that she was not alone, that there were many like her who go through similar circumstances. Some break down and give up, while others, like Aarti, rise above their adversities with their hard work, perseverance, and dedication. Neeti immediately started working on her resumé. This was the silver lining to her dark cloud that she wanted to hold on to as tightly as she could.

Neeti applied for the position and waited patiently thereafter. She knew that working for this health system was a dream for many and she was aware that there were hundreds of potential candidates who had applied for this one open position. After a few days, she received an email intimating to her that she was shortlisted for an interview and was called for one for the open position soon after. She was also told that she would be interviewing with three different people in order to get assessed for three different kinds of skillsets. Neeti was unsure if she would get this job because being a good fit for the position was not the only thing that was required in her case. Offering her a position would mean sponsoring her work visa, which was a labour-intensive process, and she was uncertain if anyone in the office even knew about what the process entailed. She trusted her capabilities but was also cognizant of the procedural hurdles because of her visa situation. She did not want to have any false hopes.

'Do you think they will sponsor my work visa,' Neeti asked Mihir the night before the interview.

'You don't know what an asset you would be to the team. Trust me, if they can, they will,' he assured her.

'Am I really an asset?'

'A high-performing one, and also high maintenance,' Mihir laughed. Neeti gave Mihir a look.

'Don't overthink, just give it your best shot and let the organization decide on the visa front. Sleep now so that you are prepared for the interview tomorrow,' Mihir said warmly.

The next morning Neeti wore a black formal dress and showed up at the office at her usual time. Her interview was scheduled for 11 a.m. but she reached at 8.45 a.m., her usual time to report to work. She finished one of the projects she was working on before the interview and at about 10.45 a.m. went to the office where her first interview was scheduled to be conducted.

This interview was with Jason Smith, the manager who had interviewed her for the volunteering position as well. Jason had faith in Neeti's talent and also admired her work ethic. He was extremely supportive and had encouraged Neeti to apply for this position, as he knew she possessed the skillsets required for the job. Jason was known and profoundly appreciated in the office for his magnanimous and philanthropic outlook. He never shied away from offering a helping hand, whether it was work-related or general guidance. He spent his weekends preparing and distributing meals to the homeless.

'What are your weaknesses, Neeti? I already know your strengths, but I would like you to tell me what your weaknesses are,' Jason probed.

'I am too detail-oriented. I know it is a strength, but at times I feel I want my work to be perfect, and I think that puts tremendous pressure on me. I want to work on that aspect,' Neeti replied.

'Do you know that perfect is the enemy of done?'

'Wow, this sums up what I was trying to say.'

Neeti then went for the other two interviews. The second one was with another manager and the last one was conducted in the afternoon, it was with the assistant director of the team and the technical details of the job were discussed during the interview. Then they all gathered together and discussed HR-related issues and details about the institution. Neeti listened patiently and also became increasingly anxious about her work authorization. Once she was asked if she had any questions, she gathered all her courage and dealt with what she thought was the elephant in the room.

'I am on a dependent visa and the organization would have to sponsor my work visa if I get offered this position,' Neeti said, being almost certain that this would abruptly end any further discussions, and could feel her heart thumping loudly.

'We know that. You did specify that in the online application. Also, we do it for many international students who get offered positions after they finish interning for us, so we have extensive experience in dealing with the paperwork regarding work visas,' the assistant director explained.

Neeti was pleasantly surprised and awfully relieved to learn that the interviewers were aware of her work authorization situation and that everything got clarified at an early stage, in case she would be offered the position.

'Do you have any other questions?'

'No, that would be all.'

She was content with her interview. All the interviewers were happy with her credentials and work experience, and they had also seen her work ethic for the last three months. She was not entirely confident that she would get the job as there were three other applicants for the same position who were called for the interview. She continued volunteering and kept going to work as usual every day. After about a month, Jason called Neeti in his office.

'Congratulations, you got the job! Here's your offer letter,' Jason said.

Neeti couldn't believe it. She was going to be on her work visa! She was ecstatic.

'But you cannot start until your work visa formality is done,' Jason continued.

'Thank you. Thank you so much! I don't know what to say,' Neeti was speechless.

'Don't say anything. Go celebrate. You won't be able to come to office for volunteering, now that your work visa is under process. So, before leaving tonight, gather all the stuff and we will see you again very soon, as one of the employees of the company!' Jason said with a smile. Just three months ago, Neeti was a housewife and a dependent; she thought she had no identity of her own. She was her husband's dependent wherever she went, and now suddenly, she had a job offer, she was not dependent on her husband anymore. She could work! All this was happening like a dream and it made Neeti think about the many women who come to the US from India on dependent visas and never get an opportunity to get a work visa. They remain housewives for the rest of their lives.

'Aarti, I got the job,' Neeti said gleefully.

'I knew it! Now I won't have to convince you to get the plants on World Environment Day! Just kidding, I am really happy for you. I have been there, done that, and I can feel every single thing you must be going through right now. Go home and celebrate!' Aarti hugged Neeti.

Neeti went back home and Mihir also took some time off work and they went to Fell's Point to celebrate this big win. They went to their favourite restaurant and celebrated Neeti's accomplishment with crab cakes and ice cream. Thereafter, they went to the waterfront and sat on a bench to watch the setting sun.

'I almost feel guilty about it,' Neeti said.

'Guilty about getting a job? Why is that?' Mihir asked.

'Pragya and many other women have been trying hard for years and I got a job in a few months.'

'Maybe you tried hard, and maybe they didn't. Maybe they don't have credentials like you, or maybe you are just luckier than them. It could be anything. But you don't need to feel guilty about it.'

'It's difficult for me to imagine that they aren't trying hard enough. I have talked to a few women and I know that they put in all the effort they could but only got disappointment in return. I wish all the spouses on dependent visas could work. I'm almost certain that most of them want to work. It's just that the process is so gruelling, with no defined timelines, that most of them just give up trying after a while.'

'I understand that, but rules are rules and there is a reason those rules are in place. I know they are probably not in the best interest of the dependent spouses and it's a shame that some really qualified people have to sit at home while their degrees gather dust hidden in the drawers. But I am positive and hopeful that the rules will change in future.'

'I hope they do. I got lucky and got in touch with a team that was supportive. It was all because of this team that I have this job today, not everyone gets an opportunity like this. I'm immensely happy and eternally grateful that I have this job now and I'm no more a dependent, and I can contribute to society and also to the household income. But deep down inside, I know that I was not able to deal with the pressure and stigma that came with being a housewife. I felt ridiculed, lowly, and worthless. I despised myself for getting those thoughts but I just could not defy myself. For all those months when I was not working, there was only one thought in my mind, "How do I start working again?"

'I know I failed as a housewife. I could not do it for even a few months, and there are so many women who spend their entire lives as housewives. A lot of employed women look down upon housewives and a lot of men think that housewives sit at home the entire day and watch soap operas on TV and gossip over the phone. In the last few months, I realized that being a housewife was nothing but hard work. You work from morning until night, without getting paid for it, and at the end of the day, people call you "unemployed", "without work", or simply "stay-at-home wife". People even use the term housewife to define your status, intelligence, and IQ.

'The entire perception of a housewife that our society has created is almost stigmatic. We don't want to become housewives because we don't want to deal with the stigma that comes along with it. We don't have the energy to respond to every single person who questions our abilities and aptitude. A housewife's opinion is not considered as important as someone's who is employed, no matter how well-read or intellectually capable she is, because she stays at home, doing "nothing", and therefore is not capable to add value to anything. Her place is in the kitchen and the biggest compliment she can get is that she is a "MasterChef", and that should make her happy and content with her life because that is all that she probably needs.

'This stigma is the reason why any woman who believes that she is strong and independent and is a housewife states clearly in her interactions that she "chose" to be a housewife. We have even come up with the fancy term "homemaker" as a little bonus to housewives, to make them "feel better". How easily we forget the contributions that housewives make to the economy. Their contributions may not be visible but their impact is felt by the entire household. This is exactly why we have the concept of imputed cost in economics. But we don't think about all this when we describe ourselves as housewives; we are either in defensive mode or in a sacrificial avatar, and honestly, some women just accept it that they are indeed lowly "housewives".

'My personal experience is a testimony to the fact that the work of housewives doesn't get its due. During the short span of time I was home, trying to be a housewife, I dealt with demeaning smug smiles to assumptions that were far removed from the realities of being a housewife that only contributed to my self-doubts leading to the erosion of my self-esteem.' Neeti's eyes welled up.

'I know you have been through a lot in the last few months, and I feel that it's all because of my decision to move to the US. I know it's not easy being a housewife and they need to be treated with much more respect than they get for all that they do. Society needs to be more vocal about the contributions that housewives make to the economies' gross domestic product. Housewives are as important as any other professional, and household work is as important as any work one does in an office. It is high time people acknowledged this and gave housewives their due,' Mihir said as he gave Neeti a hug.

***

The paperwork for Neeti's work visa got completed in six months and she started working soon after. She called her parents and gave them the big news.

'And you were doubting your capabilities all along,' Aseem said.

'I wasn't doubting my capabilities, it's just that there are rules here for everything. Although I have a work visa now, that's only for six years. I am just hoping that either Mihir or I will get our green card before the six-year limit on my work visa expires.'

'Don't worry, everything will work out fine. For now, just focus on the present,' Neeti's parents said.

She also called Rhea and told her about her work authorization. Rhea was relieved that her workaholic friend was finally getting her due.

7

Looking Ahead

With a background in finance, Neeti was able to pick things up straight off in her new role, and the team provided on-the-job training as well. Neeti knew most of the people in the team but now she was working with them as an employee and not a volunteer anymore so there was much greater involvement and participation that was expected of her. Her team made procurement decisions for the health system; this was the first time that Neeti was working in this field and she was thrilled at this opportunity.

The days were packed with meetings with the team, other departments within the health system, and with vendors. Most days she would travel to different campuses for discussions regarding capital acquisitions. As soon as she started working with the team, she started taking initiative to make presentations and do negotiations, which she was not able to do when she was working as a volunteer. She felt exhilarated

Considering that most of Neeti's acquaintances who had come to the US from India upon getting married were struggling to acquire work visa, this job meant a lot to Neeti. Mihir was still working as a post-doctoral fellow in his current lab but made Neeti aware that they might have to move out of Baltimore once he was ready to apply for assistant professorship. That was not something to be bothered about immediately, but Neeti recognized that if they moved out of Baltimore, she might have to struggle to get another job because she would need a sponsor for her work visa again. Those who come to the US to study find it easier to get a job afterwards. That implied that if Neeti had a US-based degree, she probably would not have to struggle as much to get a job even if they moved to any other city in the country. She was now on an H1-B visa and could go to school in the evening while working her day job, and she still had her valid LSAT scores. Going to law school was expensive but she was now earning enough to afford the tuition.

'I have a job now, and I am not entirely sure if I should still go to law school,' Neeti told Mihir one day.

'It would be taxing on your body and mind with a full-time job,' Mihir countered.

'I am lucky that I secured my work visa and a fulfilling job. Many people are making every effort to get work authorization and aren't able to, but I also recognize that having a law degree will probably help me get a job if we moved out of Baltimore. I was fortunate to have met extremely kind and gracious people here who saw my potential and offered me a position. I might not get this lucky somewhere else. A law degree from the US will hopefully make my job search easier in the future.'

'I totally agree with that, and I have seen you without a job, and trust me I have never seen you more lifeless ever.'

'But will it all be worth it?'

'Attaining education is always worth it. Honestly, even if you decide to never work again after getting your law degree, this investment would still be absolutely worth it.'

'You are right, but if I don't apply to law school, we can save some money and buy a house.'

'We will buy a house after your graduation. We have our whole life to buy a house.'

'Fair enough. I will start working on the application.'

Going to law school meant getting insurance for the future, insurance that came at a high premium. It would not only cost a considerable amount of money but would also require extreme levels of hard work and commitment. Neeti had a full-time job, she would have to go to school in the evenings and work on assignments during weekends. Going to law school in a country you had not studied before also came with several other challenges, you would have to understand the system, get used to the school environment, and learn the history of the country because laws evolve over time and learning the country's history is essential to appreciate its laws. Neeti had to do a tremendous amount of mental preparation before she even revisited the law school application that she had put on hold. She updated her personal statement, reached out to her mentors for recommendation letters, and started putting together the application.

She spent many nights working on her application as she was at work during the day. Weekends were spent sending reminders to people she had reached out to for recommendation letters and also preparing for the work week ahead. After weeks of hard labour, her application was finally ready. She applied to the school she wanted to go to and then the waiting game began. Every day after coming back from work, she would check her email in the hope of receiving that coveted one from the law school. Finally, an email arrived in her inbox from the law school. Not the email she was expecting, but an email that gave her hope—she was waitlisted. She was not entirely disappointed, but wished she were selected. Being waitlisted is a tricky situation; you don't feel bad because it is not rejection, but you cannot celebrate either because you aren't selected yet. 'Rhea would have cracked a joke for the situation I am in,' Neeti thought.

She went back to the online forum that she had joined at the time of taking her LSAT and read about waitlists. She learned that it was important that you showed that you were really interested in pursuing a degree from the school you had applied to so that they could confirm you. This gave Neeti some confidence. She was not entirely out of the race. All she needed to do was keep the faith and let the school know how badly she wanted a law degree from this school. She wrote to the school and scheduled an appointment with the Director of Admissions. She took the first half off from work and went for her meeting at the law school. Although she had been to the law school before for an open-house, when she stepped inside that day, it felt different. As she stepped on the large balance embossed on the marble flooring at the entrance, she felt a subtle happiness in the possibility that she could be a student in the incoming batch. The hope that she might be able to go to this law school warmed her heart. She greeted the lady at the reception and asked her for the office of the Director of Admissions.

'Hi, Neeti. Have a seat,' a very cordial Director of Admissions welcomed her with a warm smile.

'Thank you,' Neeti said as she pulled the chair to sit.

'So, you wanted to meet me. Tell me what brings you here?' the Director asked.

'I wanted to meet you to let you know how much this degree would mean to me. I have work experience of more than seven years in the field of finance and law enforcement, and this degree would match perfectly with my experience. I am not eligible for any federal funding. I will work during the day and attend classes in the evening so that I can pay for my education. I am genuinely serious about pursuing a Juris Doctor from this school as it is one of the most prestigious law schools in the country. I assure you that I will be a sincere student and will never let you or the school down.'

'That's good to know, I am pleased to see your sincerity and determination towards the law degree. My advice would be to formally write a letter of continued interest to the school so that we can consider it in the committee meeting where we will confirm some of the waitlisted candidates. Good luck to you.'

'Thank you, I appreciate that you could give your precious time to meet me.'

Neeti was glad to have met with the Director of Admissions and knew that now a sincere and concrete letter of continued interest might just help her get in. She went back to her office, finished her work, and immediately started working on the letter once she was home. She sent the letter of continued interest to the school and waited patiently for a response.

She desperately checked the mailbox every single day, and then one day, finally, a letter from the law school arrived in the mail. She had a habit of keeping the mail in the little temple at home, but she was curious and tried reading what the letter contained, from outside the envelope. But she told herself to wait. She went upstairs, kept the mail in the small temple inside, said a quick prayer, and opened the letter. Neeti had made it to the confirmed list of students. She was over the moon. She would go to the law school of her choice, the only law school she had applied to! She called Mihir and gave him the big news.

'Congratulations! Who could have said no to a candidate like you?'

'You are forgetting that I was waitlisted.'

'Please accept that you are awesome.'

'I will when I get there. Don't ever forget that I miserably failed at being a housewife, something that many around me are excelling at.'

'I think you should get over it.'

'I will try.'

'Let's celebrate your success. Be ready, I will pick you up at 6.30 p.m. and we'll go out for dinner.'

'Sounds like a plan!'

Mihir and Neeti went to a French restaurant which they fancied many times on the way to their apartment.

'I am letting you take me to this expensive restaurant only because we have something big to celebrate today. We can't splurge like this.'

'We haven't splurged ever. All we have done since the time we have gotten married is plan for the future and work hard towards it. I know the restaurant is expensive, but you deserve this. We will neither have the time nor the money to do it once you start going to school. So, for this one day, just forget everything else and enjoy your success,' Mihir said cheerfully.

Neeti wore a wine-coloured dress and Mihir wore a suit, which was a rare thing because being a lab rat, he was always in his jeans, t-shirt, and sneakers. Although they both steered clear from alcohol for the most part, that day they celebrated Neeti's admission to law school with a bottle of wine.

***

Neeti had spent almost a year working at her new position now. She was getting a hang of things but work was getting hectic and she was starting law school as well. Her classes started at 6.30 p.m., so she needed to make sure she finished all her day's work by 6, which was not easy most of the time. But she did not want to compromise on either her work or her classes. So, she had to be focused and mindful of her time and timelines.

'Take a nap at the back of the class, there is still five minutes for the class to start. I take a nap here every day, else I would collapse,' Bill, Neeti's classmate informed.

'That's a great idea!'

Neeti began taking power naps every day before the class, mostly on the way while sitting on the passenger seat as Mihir drove to her school. Most days the classes would end at around 10 p.m. Mihir would pick Neeti up from school and then they would have dinner and go to bed, getting themselves ready for the next work-day. The good thing about attending evening school was that everyone in the class was equally exhausted after the day's work but still participated eagerly in the class discussions. That inspired Neeti to give more than her 100 per cent to both her work and school.

The first year of law school is brutal. Some students don't even survive the ordeal and drop out in the first year as they find it difficult to cope with the pressure. You curse yourself, the school, and the entire universe for having taken the decision to walk on embers every day. The most difficult courses are included in the curriculum as the core courses, and they are mandatory for the first-year students. They create the very foundation on which you build your entire career as a lawyer. The first year is also ruthless because grading is done on a curve; answering a question correctly is just not enough, your grades depend on how much better your answer is in comparison to the other answers. Even if your answer is correct, if another student has provided a better answer, they will score better than you. The more such answers, the worse your grade would be. A perfectly correct answer which could have fetched you a perfect score could mean a 'C' if there were better answers from other students when the grading is done on a curve. Most students get a rude shock in the first year because everyone who is able to enroll in a law school is a bright student, but suddenly you are pitted against a hundred other bright students in the same class. Competition is intense, but the ones who break are the ones who compete with others. Once you realize that your only competition is yourself, life becomes way easier. Law school prepares you for a life as a lawyer. Your classmates aren't your competitors; they are, in fact, your colleagues and professional circle in the years to come. Once you have a clear vision, you get over the fear and anxiety that comes with attending law school.

'Would you like to present the business plan to the CFO?' Neeti's manager asked.

'I would love to,' Neeti responded.

'It's due this Monday. Be ready with all the slides and make copies for everyone who will be attending the meeting. It's Thursday today, so you have some time to work on it.'

'Sure, thank you.'

This was a huge opportunity for Neeti to showcase her talent and skills before the team and also the CFO. Her assignment for Torts was also due on Monday, so she knew that a hectic weekend was in the offing. She started working on her presentation immediately and attended her classes in the evening. She didn't have class on Friday, so she stayed back late in the office and then took her work laptop home so that she could finalize and give finishing touches to the presentation over the weekend.

'Let's order something to eat tonight. I really need to focus on finishing my presentation,' Neeti announced.

'Sure, I was going to do that. But don't you have an assignment due on Monday? Are you sure you would be able to work on both the things over the weekend? Can't you ask your professor to give you some extra time?' Mihir asked.

'I need to make a presentation to the CFO on Monday, so I want to finish it tonight. Once that's done, I can focus on the assignment. I have already made an outline for it, and it won't take me more than a day to complete it.'

'Okay, but make sure you get some rest in between.'

'I will,' Neeti said, gulping down a glass of juice to keep herself hydrated and sane.

Her presentation went well and she was able to submit her assignment on time. Since she had admirable presentation skills, she was asked to make several other presentations and she excelled at each one of them. An assignment was due every Monday that semester, so she conditioned herself to work all seven days of the week.

'It feels like we meet only in the car, and here too you end up taking naps. At all other times you are busy working. We haven't had a relaxed time to ourselves in a while.' Mihir complained.

'Someday all this hard work will pay off.'

'I hope so too.'

Neeti had made a few friends in Baltimore, but with a schedule as busy as hers, she had lost touch with most of them, so she decided to meet Pragya one Friday evening. Pragya came over and called Neeti to let her know that she was outside the main entrance to the apartment complex. One of the most important things Neeti learned after moving to the US was that you couldn't just get up and decide to go to someone's house as you did back home. You have to let people know in advance that you would be paying a visit because all apartment complexes are secure and locked, and you can't enter unless the person you were visiting opens the door to the main entrance for you. She picked up the phone and let Pragya know that she was coming down to open the main door. She went downstairs and let Pragya in.

'How's everything? I'm meeting you after such a long time,' Pragya exclaimed.

'Things are insanely busy. I didn't realize before getting myself into this.'

'I can imagine. Law school in itself is a lot to manage, and you are going to school along with a full-time job. At times I think about you and I can't make up my mind if I should feel proud of you or should feel bad that you have too much on your plate.'

'I'm doing this to secure my future. I'm not strong like you, I cannot be a housewife, I need to work professionally, and a law degree will help me get a job if Mihir and I move out of Baltimore.'

'I know, but what you are doing is not easy.'

'Being a housewife isn't easy either. You have a household to manage, you have a child to raise and are expecting another one soon. I think you need to give yourself more credit than you probably do.'

'Who really cares about household work?'

'Just because nobody does, doesn't mean it's not important, and honestly, I couldn't even do it. I failed at it miserably, and people admire me as a professional. How ironic is that!'

'This is how the world operates. You and I can do very little about it.'

'Maybe we can do much more than we think we can.'

'I have stopped thinking about it.'

'I never will.'

'Many women here are looking for work. They find it difficult to get companies who can sponsor their work visas. You are one of the very few lucky ones.'

'Yes, I realize it, and that makes me feel guilty, to be honest.'

'There is nothing to feel guilty about. I find household work to be satisfying, I take pride in it, no matter what others think of it.'

'I am glad you do. This gives me hope.'

'I deal with those demeaning questions every day and also the assumption that I married someone who lived in the US to get a life of luxury. We all know that life here is difficult if you don't have a job. It gets awfully lonely at times because you don't have the kind of neighbourhoods we enjoy back home. You don't go to someone's place unannounced. At times I feel it's good we don't get house helps here easily. At least the chores keep me occupied during the day.'

'But this is the choice we made. Maybe it was not an informed decision because we did not know about the realities of life on a dependent visa. We should have done a thorough research about life in the US for people on dependent visas. Perhaps then we would have been better prepared for it. I would not have changed my decision, but maybe I would have been a little more ready to face the consequences of my decision.'

'I wish someone had told me about these things earlier.'

'I feel the same way.'

'You are doing way better than most of us.'

'I'm just trying like everyone else. I'm proving out to be luckier than most, and that's not entirely bankable. Things have worked out for me so far but there is always uncertainty concerning your future when you are on a visa. Oh, before I forget to ask, you were trying for some volunteering positions—any progress on those?'

'Nothing has worked out for me so far, and now my delivery date is approaching, so I am not even trying too hard at this point.'

'Oh, okay. It feels weird that we spend so much time talking about visa and related issues. It feels like these problems always loom around our head. Maybe next time we meet, we should talk about something else.'

'I think so too.'

After Pragya left, Neeti kept deliberating if women who came to the US after getting married accepted it as their fate that they could not find a sponsor for their work visas, or if they got tired of looking for one. She did not have an answer, but she looked up online and found many articles on the woes of women on H-4 visas, a dependent visa category in which you are not allowed to legally work in the US. Some of the women on H-4 visas are highly qualified and have a tremendous amount of work experience. She was not sure how they dealt with it and how they came to terms with staying home all day after working professionally for long periods of time back in India.

8

Devastated

With an extremely frenzied schedule and fully packed days, time flew by in a jiffy. It was Neeti's last year of law school and sixth year of working in the US. She had become so used to this life now that at times she would wonder what she would do after finishing school. She also needed to decide if she would continue working with the health system after graduating from school or would get into the field of law immediately after graduation. Her current work profile was exciting, but she had also enjoyed the coursework and assignments in school and could not wait to get started with her legal career. Therefore, she was conflicted if she should stick with her current job, or look for opportunities with a law group. It bothered her sometimes that she had not tried getting any exposure to law-related work so far, but with a full-time job, it was not possible for her to get any internships with any law firm or group.

She was, however, getting some projects that involved working on contracts and was interacting with the legal teams within the organization. That gave her some satisfaction and assurance to try and get more work relating to contracts in future, at least there was one area of law that she could build a career in, even if she decided to stay with her current company. Leaving a job that had a healthy work environment, friendly co-workers, and engaging projects was the last thing on her mind. It was a regular day at work when Neeti got a text from Aarti.

'Hi, Neeti. Do you have a minute? It's kind of urgent.'

'Hi, Aarti. Are you okay?'

'Yes and no. Meet me whenever you have some time.'

'Sure, let me send this email out and then I can talk to you. Would you like to meet me in the break room?'

'Yes, that would work.'

Neeti sent out the email and then went to the break room to meet Aarti.

'What's the matter? You look so gloomy. Is everything all right?' Neeti grew concerned after looking at Aarti's pale face.

'No, things aren't all right.'

'What happened? Everything okay with your family?'

'Yes, no personal problems. It's something work-related, more precisely work-authorization related. My work visa is expiring soon. Has your supervisor talked to you about the green card application yet?'

'My supervisor seems to be fine with filing a green card application. Are you facing any issues?'

'Yes, my application got rejected. I will have to leave the company in fifteen days.'

'Wait, let me understand this. Your green card application was filed but it got rejected? I remember you telling me that the office is working on the application, I thought everything was going smoothly. What happened suddenly? Do you know the reason why it happened?'

'Yes, the same reason Rashmi's application got rejected. She works in the billing department.'

'I know Rashmi, I have worked with her and talk to her often. This is news to me. Her green card application got rejected too? She has bought a house, she was paying her monthly installments based on her salary, and she is enrolled in a course as well. How will she pay for all that?'

'She is devastated. She is exploring the possibilities of getting into a PhD programme.'

'But what was the reason for the rejection?'

'For your green card application, the company needs to prove that you are the only person they could find for the position that you are currently working at. For that, they need to post the position on their website, and if they get any applications from American candidates that fit the job description, the office cannot prove that they could not find a domestic candidate eligible for the job. My application got rejected internally by the Office of International Services, even before it could reach the government authorities.'

'Is that the reason for Rashmi's application being rejected too?'

'Yes, it was the same reason for the rejection of her application as well. I believe the office will now get very picky about filing green card applications in light of all these rejections.'

'Oh, but when I spoke to my supervisor, she was willing to go ahead with my application. We have not contacted the Office of International Services yet.'

'I hope things work out for you. For me and Rashmi, things turned out to be pretty rough.'

'And what are you planning to do?'

'I have no plans. I am going back to India until my husband gets his green card.'

'Let me know if you need anything, and don't let it break you. I know it is easier said than done, but trust me, something or the other will work out. I have known you for a long time, and you are a strong and resilient woman. This is just a tiny hurdle in your path of becoming a successful professional. You have your master's degree now and you will get a better position the moment you get your work authorization again.'

'I appreciate your kind words, Neeti. At the moment, I just want to take a break from all this mess and spend some time with my folks back home. I'm finding it difficult to come to terms with it. But I just want you to be prepared if something like this happens with you.'

Neeti hugged Aarti and she broke down. Neeti could feel her pain but did not know what she could do to ease it. Words could only help so much. She just hoped and prayed that Aarti's husband got his green card soon so that Aarti could start working again.

Neeti had been absolutely comfortable with the idea that once her work visa was about to expire, the office would file for a green card and she would not have to worry about losing her job, but after hearing about what happened to both Aarti and Rashmi's green card applications, she was not sure if her application would get accepted. Rashmi was at a managerial position. If the office could not prove that she was the only one they could find eligible for the position and there were no domestic candidates eligible for the job that she was doing, it would be difficult to prove that Neeti was the only one that the office found eligible for the position of a senior analyst. Neeti was now concerned about Rashmi and also herself. She met Rashmi the next morning and talked to her at length.

'I had no idea that your green card application was rejected. Aarti told me about it yesterday. Why did you not tell me?'

'The more I talk about it, the worse I feel. I didn't expect my application to get rejected. This is just so disappointing. This job was more than just a job for me, I started my career here, and this was my first job. I came to this country for my master's degree and finished it with honours. I even did my internship here with this company before I was hired as a full-time employee. I joined as an analyst and worked my way up the managerial level in just a few years. I am emotionally connected to this place, it is not easy for me to cut the ties one fine morning, forgetting all this. I understand the practical reasons, the laws, everything, but I cannot come to terms with it.'

'I don't know what to say, I have been thinking about you and Aarti since the time she told me about all this.'

'Thanks, Neeti, but honestly, this is not something a third person can feel. What we are going through is not something we can express in words.'

'I am sorry you have to go through this.'

'Have you talked to your supervisors yet?'

'I have, and I was under the impression that these applications go through smoothly. Now I'm nearing my six-year limit on the visa, and I'm not sure if my application will go through either.'

'You have a different role than what I had. You never know, something miraculously could turn in your favour.'

'That's the hope I have too.'

'What are you planning to do now?'

'I have decided to switch to a student visa and enroll in a PhD programme.'

'I am glad at least you have a plan B, and I sincerely hope things work out for you.'

'Thanks, Neeti, and good luck to you. I hope you don't have to go through what I am going through.'

Neeti was still trying to make sense of everything that was happening around her. Two of her colleagues who had been working with her for many years, were about to lose their jobs and also their work authorization soon, despite the fact that they were hardworking, sincere, and one of them was a star performer. The laws did not have any leniency for the hardworking. Once your work authorization reaches the maximum limit, you have no option but to leave. It was unsettling, but Neeti did not want to overthink. She instead wanted to act on it as soon as possible. So, she decided to talk to her supervisor, Susan Morgan.

'Hi, Susan. Do you have some time this week? I had a couple of queries regarding my green card application.'

'Yes, I have been meaning to talk to you about that as well. Why don't we meet on Wednesday afternoon? Could you send me a meeting invite?'

'Sure.'

Neeti went to Susan's office on Wednesday afternoon and asked her if the office could start her green card application as it was a labour-and-time-intensive process.

'Would you like me to get in touch with the Office of International Services or would you like to take the lead on it?'

'I can get in touch with them and can update you.'

'Sounds good.'

Neeti got in touch with the Office of International Services and they told her that they would contact Susan shortly. Neeti's work authorization was to expire in six months. She was on an H1-B visa, a non-immigrant visa allowing foreign nationals to temporarily work in the US, based on their skills. The maximum you can work under this visa category is six years. A green card or permanent residency allows you to continue to stay and work in the US indefinitely. Therefore, when your work visa is about to reach its maximum limit, companies try to file for green cards for their employees so that they can continue working legally in the US.

A few days passed since she had received the email from the Office of International Services and Neeti was starting to get extremely anxious. She decided to send an email to Susan asking about the updates. Susan called Neeti to her office as soon as she received Neeti's email.

'Hi, Susan. Can I come in?'

'Hi, Neeti. Please do, have a seat.'

'I was just wondering if the Office of International Services got in touch with you.'

'I actually wanted to call you and talk about it but the new project that I am working on kept me extremely occupied, but I would have apprised you with the updates either today or tomorrow. So, I am glad you sent me an email inquiring about this. The Office of International Services did get in touch with me. In fact, we've had more than a couple of conference calls and meetings. We were discussing all the issues and details relating to the process of filing for a green card. The application is labour-intensive and the Office of International Services is taking each case very seriously and assessing the merits of the case before putting in the time, effort, and money in the process.

'After many days of deliberations and discussions, our team and the Office of International Services finally have decided that it will not be feasible to file for a green card for you because its application will not get approved, given the circumstances. One of the requirements for getting a green card for someone working at your position is that no other domestic candidate is eligible for the position and that a green card would be required so that the international candidate can continue working at the position.

'The Office of International Services also told me about the cases that they have recently rejected because they could not prove that the international candidate was the only one they could find eligible for the position, and a lot of effort goes into the application even before a position is posted to assess if there are domestic candidates available for the position. So, they are screening every application at the outset. We discussed the possibility of filing a green card for you and what it would entail. We will have to post your position and prove to the United States Citizenship and Immigration Services that you were the only candidate we could find eligible for the job you are doing.

'You are working as a senior analyst, and one posting for this position would get hundreds of applicants, and many of them would have the required experience and skillset to do the job. It would be impossible for us to prove that you are the only person who is eligible to do this job and hence you need a green card. Therefore, the argument that you need and deserve a green card because you are the only candidate the office found eligible for this position would not hold ground. It is a collective decision to not go ahead with filing the petition for a green card for you because the process is enormously arduous, and when the outcome is already known, it makes little sense to go down that path. It is certainly disheartening, not only for you but also for the team, and everyone is distraught by the decision.'

'I understand,' Neeti managed to utter with a lump in her throat.

'Neeti, I know it is difficult for you to deal with this, and there was no easy way for me to convey it to you. I can assure you that I tried my best to convince the Office of International Services that you are the best candidate for the position, but the requirement is only for someone eligible, not the best.

My hands are tied, and I am as disappointed as you are, if not more. Finding someone like you for this position would be very difficult, and losing an employee like you is a loss for the organization, but rules are rules and we cannot break them.'

'I trust you, Susan, and I am thankful to you for trying so hard. I appreciate your kind words. It would be difficult to deal with it but I will try my best and I will start wrapping up my projects and prepare for the transition of my duties.'

'Please feel free to discuss anything you want with me, and don't hesitate to ask any questions. I want to help you in every possible way.'

'Thanks, Susan. It means a lot.'

Neeti came back to her office and went blank. She did not know how to react to this. After she got to know that her colleagues' green card applications had got rejected, she knew that there was a possibility of her application getting rejected too, but even then, she hoped against hope that things would work out for her. She sat on her chair and after some time she realized that she had been staring at her computer screen for about five minutes. She could not think of anything, she just went numb.

The next couple of months were extremely challenging for Neeti, more so because she was in denial. When you are in denial, you don't see things as they are. You keep hoping unreasonably and don't want to accept the truth. She was not ready to accept that she was about to lose her job as well as the possibility of getting another job for an uncertain period of time, for no fault of hers. She was a hardworking employee and had been working sincerely throughout her career. She had the required qualification and also the skillset for the job and despite that, she was being asked to stop working because the laws of the country required her to do so.

Acceptance came at a huge price. She would cry every day, even in the office. Her team and colleagues empathized with her, but they were helpless. After days of crying, getting livid at small issues, and getting irritated, Neeti eventually resigned to reality and got out of the denial phase. Working professionally had been a part of Neeti's identity for a very long time now, and she was feeling as if someone was snatching away that part of her. She wanted to feel whole but nothing was helping. Her skin began to break out, her face looked pallid, and she lost five kilos in the last couple of months. She looked at herself in the mirror one day and started crying profusely. She was getting consumed by her sadness. It needed to stop.

'I will never be able to work again and it hurts,' Neeti told Mihir one day, fighting her tears.

'Trust your talent and skills more than you mistrust your destiny,' Mihir tried to comfort her.

'I don't know what to trust and what to mistrust now, everything looks like a haze.'

'You have worked hard all your life. You cannot give up like this now,' Mihir hugged Neeti.

'I can't fight the unknown. There is no certainty about anything. I don't know if there is anything I can even try to do at this point. When I came here after getting married, at least I had hope of getting a work visa. Now I can do absolutely nothing until you get your green card. I have never felt so helpless in life.'

'You are not helpless. Things will not remain like this forever. Keep the faith. I am going to apply for my green card and you would be able to get your work authorization as soon as we get approval. I am not saying that it will happen right away, and I am not denying that this phase isn't difficult…'

'Words aren't helping, Mihir. People want to work because it makes them feel that they are contributing to society. It gives them a feeling of belongingness, that they have the skills to make this world a better place, and they want to make the world a better place to live by using their skillsets. But when you are told that you can no longer continue, you feel cut off from the very society you were a part of. You feel restrained. It's not just a loss of work authorization, it's a loss of independence. Every time someone loses their work authorization, it not only deprives them of working, but also breaks them financially, mentally, and emotionally.'

'These aren't empty words. I am working on my green card application.'

'I don't see any light at the end of this tunnel.'

'You need to open your mind when some doors close. If you keep thinking about your work authorization, you will not be able to think about other things that are probably more important than your work authorization—your health, for example.'

Mihir's words made little sense to Neeti. All she wanted was to vent. 'I am aware that I had chosen to come to this country of my own will and I knew about the possibility of this happening when the same thing happened to my colleagues. Many people who had come from India to the US, just like I did, did not even get work or work authorization, to begin with. Despite knowing all this, I wish the rules weren't this brutal, they should have some consideration for the qualification, experience, and skillsets of people on visas, give a little more importance to their sincerity and hard work, and treat them with more compassion.'

'It's okay to cry, but it's not okay to lose hope. I can't see you like this. I will start working on the green card application right away. Just be a little patient.'

This was not the first time Neeti burst into tears like this. It was an everyday occurrence since she came to know that her green card application would not be processed and she would lose the legal right to work in this country. Mihir hugged her until she stopped crying. The thought of losing her work authorization was killing her from inside. It was a pain that was too difficult to explain. For others, it was just that she would not be able to work for some time; some even told her that now she would get time to have fun and enjoy life without being bothered about working. But for Neeti, it was losing her financial independence, her professional interactions, and most importantly, the right to work professionally, which had been a part of her identity for as long as she could remember.

Suddenly, one day, the crying stopped, the irritability disappeared, and she went silent. The pain was too much to even talk about, and there was no point talking about it. There was a storm building inside her but she looked so calm that her colleagues started getting concerned. They kept checking on her and some suggested meditation. She signed up for websites offering yoga and meditation classes, but all in vain.

'I am sending you a link. The subscription is free for the employees. Try it out, you still have a couple of months left before the work authorization expires,' Susan said.

'Thanks, Susan. I will try.'

'Honestly speaking, I would totally enjoy this break that you are getting. Consider yourself lucky. You can use this time to pursue a hobby, reflect on your life or just relax.'

'I would have enjoyed it if it was voluntary. Right now it feels like someone is forcing me to have fun when I want to work. It's like pulling the plug on your dreams against your wishes. I will lose financial independence and professional interactions, and it has already started affecting my self-esteem.'

'You are a brave girl, Neeti. You should be the last person to think like this.'

'I thought the same way when I heard about other people losing their work authorization, but you don't know how something like this affects you until it happens to you.'

'I wish I could help.'

'You are, and thank you for everything you are doing.'

Now that it was certain that she would lose her work authorization soon, Neeti started wrapping up her projects and started working on a transition plan. She started letting all the co-workers know that she would leave soon and began holding meetings with everyone she was working with. She made sure she answered any pending questions they had on the projects she was working on. She prepared a list of pending projects that could not be completed immediately and discussed the transition plan with Susan.

'I love this transition plan, Neeti!'

'Thanks, Susan, I just wanted to make sure that it is detailed enough so that the projects don't end up suffering. I hope the next person who comes in my place can understand them through this plan.'

'We will miss you terribly.'

'I too will miss you all.'

9

The Awakening

Combining her work experience in India and the US, Neeti had been working for more than a decade now and she was not able to accept the fact that after a few months she would not be able to continue working despite being able and willing. She was about to lose her job and also the authorization to work, for no fault of hers. She was not a lousy employee, nor did she do anything wrong at work. She was just someone who was on a visa, and there are rules set by every country for the visa holders that they have to abide by. She understood that the rules were in place for a reason and every country had the right to impose these restrictions, but she was having a hard time dealing with the loss of her job and work authorization.

She had been struggling with all kinds of negative and distressing thoughts for months now. She cried, got angry, and was frustrated with the whole system. But gradually she told herself to calm down because being agitated was not helping her at all; in fact, it was harming her, she was losing weight rapidly, and was hardly getting any sleep at night. She was, however, still going to the law school and had something to look forward to. This is when she realized for the first time that going to law school probably wasn't a bad decision, after all. Because she had been going through so many different emotions, she had almost started blaming herself for going to law school.

'I could have saved all the money I invested in going to law school and maybe then I would not be feeling so bad about losing my job and work authorization,' Neeti had lamented one day.

'How much money do you think you would have been able to save? Do you think it would have lasted a lifetime? You have earned a Juris Doctor, and that *will* last for a lifetime. Do you even realize it? Besides, was money the reason you wanted to work?' Mihir had asked.

'No, not entirely. I wanted to work because working professionally is a big part of my identity. I don't feel whole unless I work, hardly matters whether I get paid for it or not.'

'Then why are you getting all these self-doubts now?'

'It seems like my whole life is falling apart.'

'You are in school and have the current and the next semester to look forward to. Focus on the things that you can do rather than the ones you have no control over.'

'That I am still in school does make me feel that I am still worthy. I know that it is foolish to get these thoughts about not being worthy enough, but I just cannot stop thinking about it.'

'You need to stop thinking like this. This attitude will kill you from inside. It's a dangerous path you are treading, stop right now,' Mihir had pleaded.

'I want to continue working!'

'You will! Consider it a break that you truly deserve. You have been working and going to school for the last five years. Why can you not take a break?'

'Because I have not decided to take this break, this break is being imposed on me.'

'You can't fight the rules, and we will get your work authorization back soon. Trust me on that, and please go easy on yourself!'

This conversation with Mihir had helped Neeti appreciate the fact that she still had something to look forward to every day and would not have to spend her days crying in a corner at home. It was a huge respite, but she wanted to continue working somehow. Getting paid for it was not important, getting up every morning and going to work was. So, during the last semester of her law school, she decided to apply for an externship—an internship where you get academic credit instead of getting paid monetarily. The externship would be full time and she would not feel that she wasn't working anymore, but instead of getting paid, she would earn academic credit. It was a win-win for her. She could use this externship to transition from being suddenly unemployed to being employed but as an extern before coming to terms with the fact that she had lost her work authorization. This would provide her the much-needed cooling period to accept the reality of her current job situation.

'Maybe it's a blessing in disguise. I will finally get to work as a law intern and work in the field that I wanted to work in for a long time, and for which I have spent so many years in school,' Neeti thought to herself.

Then she remembered that she had asked one of her classmates to provide names of some of the public interest organizations that offered externships. She looked for that email, perused the list carefully, and finalized a programme that provided legal services to families of children with disabilities. She sent an email to the team to see if they were accepting externship applications for spring and thought to herself, 'Maybe this is a start to another waiting game.' As she was about to finish her lunch break, an email popped up, which read, 'We would love to consider your externship application for spring. Please send your resume and a writing sample.'

Neeti was thrilled. She sent out her resume and a writing sample, and she was immediately called for an interview. She was elated; this was the first time she had smiled in months. She immediately started preparing for the interview. Although it was only an externship, she knew how much it meant to her, she did not want to mess this up in any way. She wore a formal dress with a jacket for the interview. The interview turned out to be more of a conversation; the team had already decided that she was being offered the externship for the spring semester. She was delighted.

Neeti had taken some time off from the office to appear for this interview, after which she returned to the office and told everyone that she had got selected for the externship. Everyone congratulated her and was happy that she would not have to sit idle at home after the expiration of her work authorization. Neeti returned home and shared the good news with Mihir.

'You know Mihir, I always wanted to work in the field of public interest, right from the time of volunteering with Prayaas, but I never got an opportunity after that. You don't choose public interest work, public interest work chooses you. Maybe I am the chosen one, finally,' Neeti said.

'You will do great!' Mihir said, cheering Neeti up.

'I hope so. The desire to work with public interest groups stems from the desire to serve the underprivileged, helping the poor, working for the public good. The weird thing about such aspirations is that all these require the world to be a bad place, to have flaws and problems so that we can make it better. So, it feels a little selfish.'

'But the world indeed is a mix of good and bad, and there are problems all around.'

'That's true. Perhaps the better way to look at it is to accept the harsh reality that poverty, disability, and oppression exist in the world, and you can contribute towards making the world a better place to live in, through public interest organizations. I felt the same way when I was volunteering for Prayaas, and I am glad we were able to make a difference to the kids through the mentorship programme. I hope I will be able to make a difference here as well.'

Neeti's work authorization was to expire on 31st October, and it was almost time and she was now mentally prepared for it. She had exams to study for and immediately thereafter was to begin her externship. Now was not the time to feel gloomy, there was too much to do and much to look forward to.

She got a warm farewell from her team and she wrote thank you notes for everyone and said her goodbyes. On her last day at work, Neeti wore red which for her was the colour of hope. She was smiling and was ready to start her journey as a law intern. For now, she had accepted that she had little control over certain aspects and was excited to work on the things that were in her control.

Neeti was on a dependent visa again. This time it was an H-4 visa as Mihir was on his H-1B visa. But she decided to completely focus on school right now. Neeti had taken two courses this semester. One of them required her to submit assignments every week and a final assignment at the end of the semester, and the other one had a final exam at the end of the semester. The due date for the final assignment was the beginning of November, which she had finished, and then she had almost a month to prepare for the last exam of her law school. Since she would be doing an externship in spring, she would not have to take any exams and would just have to submit assignments related to the externship. So, she wanted to completely focus on her last exam of law school now. She treated her days like workdays, but instead of going to office, she sat on her study desk and prepared for the exam. Preparing for the final exam kept her busy and she did not miss office as much. After the exam was over, she took a little break, and then it was the holiday season and everyone was in a festive mood. It made things a little easier for Neeti because all the festivities not only kept her busy but also happy, which was the most important thing at that time.

Neeti was now looking forward to her externship and had to get the paperwork together. She sent out all the required forms and got her work identification card. So much was happening that she did not get time to grieve her lost work authorization. Also, there was a lot to look forward to and she did not want to waste a single second ruminating about things that were beyond her control. She wanted to make the most of the present.

Mihir was well aware of Neeti's situation. He would try and cheer her up every time he saw her upset. He would tell her that she was still in school, she should focus on her externship and graduation, and these were the things she had long been waiting for. He told her that she had worked hard all these years; maybe she was getting a little break because she rightfully deserved it.

The festive season ended and so did the winter break. It was time for Neeti to turn over a new leaf and start her externship that she was eagerly waiting for. The externship was with one of the best programmes in the field of disability rights for children in the state of Maryland. The programme provided legal services to families with children with disabilities. Most of these families belonged to lower-middle to lower economic classes who were unable to afford private attorneys. The fee structure was based on a sliding scale fee-for-service model, which meant that if you earned more, you paid more; if you earned less, you paid less. Most of the families fell into the lowest brackets and some couldn't pay even the lowest rate. The programme then arranged for funding for such families.

Neeti always wanted to work in the field of public interest, even when she was working in India. Therefore, this externship meant the world to her. Two weeks into her new job and she was already in love with it.

'Neeti, we have scheduled some school tours for you tomorrow. We hope you like them. It will be a remarkable learning experience for you to go and see what these schools are doing to help children with disabilities,' Neeti's supervisor said.

'Thank you, I am looking forward to the tours,' Neeti responded.

Neeti's colleague told her that this would be a very "special" experience for her. She wasn't quite sure what her colleague was talking about, but since she knew that her colleague had a very soft side to her, Neeti truly believed that it would be special.

Neeti woke up and got ready and was excited because it was the day of school tours. She knew it was going to be a special experience, and that's all she knew about it. It was a beautiful spring day and a light breeze was blowing. The sidewalks were carpeted with yellow and magenta flowers. She was keenly looking forward to the "special experience". Neeti could not wait to begin the day. She went for the school tours. She came back home and went to use the bathroom. Half an hour later, she was still inside.

'Neeti, are you all right?' Mihir enquired.

'I am not, give me some time.' Neeti's voice was cracking.

Neeti wept and wept, and then wept some more. Her tears did not stop.

She wanted to throw up. She held on to the wash-basin and almost felt that she would pass out. She looked into the mirror and instead of seeing her face, she saw helplessness. She started to think about all that she saw during the school tours. Neeti was working with a team of lawyers who specialized in the field of special education law and helped families with children with disabilities with their legal rights to education. The right to Free, Appropriate Public Education (FAPE) is one thing that most families with children with disabilities fight for. The team helped those families in getting the children what they deserved as per the law. Appropriate education also included the right placement of the children in the schools best suited to their needs. Not every child with a disability can be served in the same school. Every child with a disability has a specialized need, and different schools cater to different kinds of needs. A severely autistic child, for example, will not benefit from going to a generic school because the needs of the child call for specialized instruction and accommodations with a smaller teacher-to-student ratio than what is usually the case in a generic school. However, if a child has mild learning disabilities, their needs can be met by making some accommodations in the general classroom, or they may be required to go to school with largely the same setup but a smaller class size. These school tours were scheduled for Neeti to help her understand the kind of disabilities that were taken into consideration by some of the specialized schools.

She first toured the high school that was for children with learning disabilities. The children looked joyful. The class sizes were smaller than the typical class sizes in a generic school. The teachers were able to pay attention to all the children in the classroom and children had various study aids to help them perform better. Although all kids had a right to study in the Least Restrictive Environment (LRE), certain disabilities made it almost impossible for some students to get the appropriate instruction in a regular classroom with other kids with no disabilities. For children with such disabilities, these special schools were the best fit. Neeti was pleased to see so many happy faces.

The senior students were also learning important life skills and were getting vocational training so that they could become self-dependent and be able to contribute to the economy. She was extremely delighted to see this. She even gave high fives to some of the students. After she was done with the tour of the high school, she was scheduled to visit a special programme for children with severe disabilities.

She thought she was ready.

She wasn't.

As soon as she entered this part of the school, she saw children with head and body gear because they would tend to harm themselves. Those kids had severe disabilities and this was the only way to protect them. Some of the kids were too young to even bear the weight of the body gear. She stood there, motionless. She looked at the kids again and suddenly felt that she had no emotions, she was numb. All she felt was helplessness engulfing her.

'Neeti, do you have any questions?' the instructor asked.

'No, I am good,' Neeti responded. There were no words that could have conveyed what she felt at that time. There was no way for her to explain what she was feeling inside, so she decided to keep quiet. She continued with the tour and saw a kid whose task for the day was to stay stable and catch a ball. Every time he did that, he was given a treat. She saw some more kids with severe disabilities and observed how the instructors cheered for them every time they completed their tasks. Every time the kids failed to complete the task, the instructor relentlessly assured them that they can do it, and encouraged the kids to go for it again. She saw this and thought to herself, the world keeps talking about bigger and better things and ideas every day, humans want to go to Mars and there are people on Earth struggling to have a basic, normal life. She couldn't bear it, she felt suffocated.

The next part of the tour was a visit to the seclusion rooms, to be used rarely and only in case the situation was such that seclusion was absolutely unavoidable. She was shown a seclusion room that had padding all around.

'Why is the room padded?' Neeti asked the instructor, breaking her silence, finally.

'Some of the kids tend to bang their heads against the walls. This is done for their safety,' the instructor explained.

Neeti saw the blue padding around the room one more time and left the room. She reached for her water bottle in her bag and had a sip. Her throat was dry and she couldn't utter another word. She thanked the staff for the tour and also for taking such good care of the children. She couldn't bear what she saw even for a day. 'How do these people make themselves go through the same emotions every single day without getting emotionally drained?' she thought. She had a newfound respect for people working in the field of disability and could not be more thankful for what they were doing.

Neeti came back home and felt heavy, it almost felt like she was carrying a burden inside her. She didn't cry.

'How did you like the school tours?' Mihir asked.

She was silent. There was nothing to talk about. 'They were okay,' she mustered all her energy to say this and then went to the bathroom and broke down.

She had been miserable for so many months because she lost her work authorization. She was physically and mentally fit, had attained education from the best of the institutes, had a loving family, and most comforts of life that a human being desires. As far as her work authorization was concerned, she would probably get it again, maybe not immediately, but at some point in future, and she had been crying for days, behaving as if her life had come to a standstill, that she had lost purpose in her life. She complained that she had lost her work authorization without being at fault. Today she had witnessed some children struggling to keep their heads straight. Forget enjoying life, they could not even walk in a straight line, and some even struggled to sit, eat, or talk. Some were prone to self-harm without having any clue about it. What was their fault? Did they do anything wrong to deserve this life? No, they were little kids who had never even hurt a fly, and they were going through things you would not wish even to the worst of your enemies. Neeti felt ashamed of herself. Her problem was miniscule in comparison to what she had seen today. It didn't mean that her problem was non-existent; it indeed was a problem, given her circumstances, but today she got a whole new perspective towards life. This school tour was life-changing. The Neeti that emerged from the tour wasn't the same person who had entered the school building in the morning.

She decided that she would not cry thinking about her work authorization anymore. Maybe her situation was bad, but she had so many other things in life to feel happy about. The key to happiness is to make the best of what you have got rather than crying over what you have lost. Those little kids were a tremendous source of inspiration. They were celebrating their small victories, every time they finished a task, they would give a hi-five to their instructor and smile. There was so much to learn from them. Neeti didn't know what the future held for her, but she decided that she would try her best to work in the field of disability law.

She loved going to work every morning. Every day the lady at the front-desk greeted her with the same warmth and Neeti never forgot to smile back at her. Because it was a public interest law group with limited funding, it wasn't a large team and there were only three attorneys and two more interns who used to come to the office only once or twice a week as per their schedule. Therefore, as soon as Neeti reached office every day, there were always a bunch of calls to attend to and parents to meet. She loved meeting and talking to parents. She felt that when she spoke to them, she gave them hope, and once you have hope, your sadness alleviates. It was gratifying to see happiness all around her, which was blooming from a surprisingly sad place of disabilities. She admired the spirit of the parents of the children with disabilities who were trying to beat their odds with a smile on their faces.

There were days when she would cry talking to parents because they would cry describing their situation and their kid's disability. She connected with each one of them. Human connections are so strong that you don't even need to know the other person; pain connects you to another human being almost instantly. She was there to help and was trying her best to reduce their pain. There is a strange peace in bringing smiles to people's faces, even if you had forgotten to smile, and in the process, you don't even realize when you learn to smile again. Neeti had found her happiness back.

'Neeti, I have an IEP meeting scheduled for today. Would you like to join me?' Neeti's supervisor, Marilyn Fiore, asked.

'Sure, I would love to,' Neeti responded.

IEP is an acronym for 'Individualized Education Program'. According to the Individuals with Disabilities Education Act (IDEA), every child with a disability is eligible to have an IEP to help them achieve their educational goals. Unfortunately, not every school qualifies a child with a disability as one because schools can do their in-house testing and the assessment is based on that testing, and even when they do qualify a child as a child with a disability, they don't always provide an IEP best suited for the child's educational requirements. When a parent sees their child regressing, they reach out to lawyers to intervene because the child is legally eligible to get an IEP best suited to their needs. IEP meetings are the ones where the school representatives meet with the parents to discuss a child's eligibility, IEP, and also placement, whether the child is placed at a school best suited to their needs. This law group catered to families with lower means, so they came with very little money and a lot of hope. Neeti was going to an IEP meeting for one such family.

'Let's go around the table and introduce ourselves,' the IEP chair said. Everyone introduced themselves and the IEP meeting officially started.

'Miss Brown, as a parent of the child, do you have any concerns?' the IEP chair asked. Miss Brown was Leila's mother. Leila was the client that Neeti's law group was representing.

'Leila is a very special kid and she is very sincere, she has been consistently regressing and now cannot even spell simple English words while other students in her class can write sentences without much difficulty,' Miss Brown said.

Everyone in the room went quiet, the silence was loud and piercing, and amidst that, one could hear Miss Brown sobbing in a low voice. Neeti reached out for a tissue paper from her bag; she didn't even realize when she herself started crying with Miss Brown.

'Would everyone want a short break, just in case anyone wants to use the restroom or have a snack? This is an early morning meeting, not sure if all of you have had your breakfast,' the IEP chair said, sensing the grim atmosphere and trying to break that deafening silence.

They took a short break and regrouped to discuss the concerns. Marilyn explained to everyone in the group; how Leila was eligible for way more services and accommodations than she was being provided currently. She needed a dedicated aide to help her during the classes and also extra time to complete both her classwork and homework. She explained the law to the group and also explained how it was important for Leila to have all those services and accommodations to achieve her educational goals. Marilyn was polite but firm. She answered the questions of the group with a detailed explanation of the law. Neeti took notes of everything.

By the end of the meeting, the school representatives agreed that there was a gap in the kind of services and accommodations that Leila was currently getting and what she needed in order to achieve her educational goals. The school then came up with a plan and discussed how new services and accommodations would be added to Leila's IEP and how her progress would be measured. The group scheduled the next meeting where the new and approved IEP would be discussed and the meeting concluded with Miss Brown beaming from ear to ear. She came and hugged both Marilyn and Neeti. Neeti was happy to see how Marilyn was able to convert Miss Brown's tears into a beatific smile. She hoped that someday she would also do the same to a family in need.

Neeti and Marilyn went back to the office to meet some more parents in need. More work meant more happiness to both Marilyn and Neeti, they looked at each other and smiled. Neeti described her day to Mihir after she returned home.

'Silent tears are the loudest,' Neeti told Mihir.

'Yes, they are, and I am so proud of the fact that you are turning those tears into smiles.'

'How was your day? Sorry, I have been dealing with so much lately. I sometimes forget to ask you about your days.'

'It's okay, you have been through a lot ever since you stepped inside this country. I'm glad you are finding happiness, finally. My day was fine. I'm finishing up writing a research paper and, hopefully, I can mention it in the green card application.'

'Would you like a peanut butter sandwich? I am making one for myself.'

'Sure.'

Every single day of her externship was a day Neeti cherished. It was one of the best periods of her life. Helping others brought her immense joy. When you help others, you help yourself, albeit unknowingly. She looked forward to each day with much enthusiasm. She was getting to meet parents and attend IEP meetings. She also met with some senators and lobbyists who were pushing for a certain bill for disability rights to be passed. She met many lawyers working in the field and every single one was an inspiration. Neeti was learning tremendously and loving it so much that she forgot that it was only a semester-long externship. She did not want to stop working there. But rules were rules, she was only allowed to work until the end of the semester.

'I'd love to continue working here. Is there any possibility I can volunteer here after graduating from school, given that I cannot work as an employee because I don't have work authorization right now?' Neeti asked Marilyn.

'Absolutely, it will be a pleasure to have you, Neeti. You can certainly volunteer with us.'

Neeti was overjoyed. To continue working with the group even after graduation was a dream come true.

It was the last day of her externship and she was excited about the volunteering opportunity. She came to work and, after finishing the day's work, thanked everyone. This externship not only changed her perspective on life but also changed her life in a way. She was content and felt positive about what she had in life rather than focusing on what she didn't. Marilyn told her to stay in touch as she was starting the paperwork for the volunteering position for Neeti.

Neeti got a perfect score on her externship and the professor overseeing it forwarded her the remarks she had received from the law group. Neeti had done exceedingly well. Now that she had successfully completed all the semesters, it was time for her graduation. A day that every student eagerly looks forward to. She tried on her graduation dress and regalia the night before the graduation day. Her dress was black with beige and purple flowers on the borders. Its bell-shaped sleeves bothered her when she bought the dress, but they soon grew on her. The graduation gown was black with purple stripes. She got two caps in the packet she ordered online: one was the regular graduation cap and the other one was the velvet doctoral tam. She looked up online for information on different kinds of graduation caps and realized that since hers was a doctoral degree, she had earned the right to choose her cap from the two that came in the packet. She finally decided to wear the tam. She was not entirely happy with the shoes she tried on. She had an irrational fear that she would fall while walking up to the stage for her hooding ceremony. It wasn't difficult to tell that she was ecstatic about her graduation.

Neeti was radiating on her graduation day. She had now learned to compartmentalize her brain. Just because you have troubles and worries doesn't mean you should stop enjoying the fruits of your labour, or stop celebrating your achievements, or stop living your life in a wholesome way. She also had realized how important it was to be grateful for what you have in life, so she wanted to make the most of her day—the day she had been waiting for.

Even when she started school, she understood what a big deal it was to pursue Juris Doctor, but on her graduation day, she saw the magnitude of it. All graduating students were dressed in academic regalia. They were gathered in the magnificent Westminster Hall and everyone was hugging and congratulating one another. The professors told them how proud they were of the graduating class. Neeti had butterflies in her stomach and tears in her eyes. They walked through the campus to reach the Hippodrome Theater where the hooding ceremony was supposed to take place, and everyone around clapped while they walked wearing their regalia and broadest smiles.

Mihir beamed with pride as he took pictures of Neeti when she got out of the car. Neeti was posing excitedly, and so was every other graduating student around her. The atmosphere brimmed with positivity and Neeti was on cloud nine. She would just not stop taking selfies. They reached the Hippodrome Theater and Neeti could not control her tears. Her name was called and she walked up to the stage, where her professor put the hood around her. Mihir watched her from a distance and felt immensely proud of what Neeti had achieved. Afterwards, they went for a long drive and spent some quality time with each other. They didn't talk much; just held hands and assured each other that they would be there for one another, no matter what.

The next day, Neeti sent her graduation pictures to her ex-colleagues including Marilyn and asked her if she could start volunteering right away. Marilyn sent her the paperwork that she was required to submit to start processing everything at their end. Neeti sent her the paperwork immediately. Two days later, she got an email from Marilyn. It read:

> Hi, Neeti,
>
> I hope you are doing well.
>
> I just got done speaking to HR and we would not be able to offer you the volunteering position. Working with our team requires you to access the health records of children with disabilities and without work authorization, we cannot allow you to access those health records. If you would not be able to access the health records, which is a critical part of determining what kind of services the children need, your functioning would be limited to a very large extent. Therefore, at this time we would not be able to onboard you as a volunteer. Having said that, please know that you have been an extremely sincere and hardworking extern and it would be a pleasure to have you over for lunch. Please keep us posted whenever you get your work authorization and we will onboard you soon after.
>
> Best Regards,
>
> Marilyn

This was totally unexpected and Neeti was not ready for this, but she took a deep breath and thought of the children she had met during the school tours, and she immediately responded:

Hi, Marilyn,
Thank you for keeping me posted. I completely understand the limitations because of my visa situation. I will keep you posted about my work authorization and will see you soon.
Thanks for all your help and guidance.
Sincerely,
Neeti

This was the last door that Neeti could see open which had just closed on her. She was blank, she did not have any other alternative plans now.

'I know it's not the end of the world, but I do feel like a failure, Mihir,' Neeti said.

'You have always said that you are a failure only when you don't try; you tried. There are rules and procedures for certain things. You cannot beat the system.'

'But I failed as a housewife too, and the work-life failed me. Where do I stand now?'

'Stop being so hard on yourself, this is just a phase. Not everything is meant for everyone. You did not fail as a housewife, you wanted to offer much more to society than just household work, and you continued taking care of the household work even after you got a job and started school. You need to start giving yourself the credit you deserve.'

'I could never become a successful housewife.'

'Many people don't become successful professionals, not everyone is the same. You conditioned yourself to be a professional from the very beginning, and there is absolutely nothing wrong with it.'

'But I am back to square one.'

'No, you are not. You have six years of work experience, a Juris Doctor, and a whole new perspective on life. Don't discount all that.'

'You think I will be able to handle it?'

'I am positive about it. You have done amazing things in life. The only thing you need to learn is to give yourself some credit and stop being overly critical of yourself.'

'Will I ever be able to become a successful housewife?'

'It depends on your definition of success. Stop comparing yourself with others, to begin with. Do what comes to you naturally.'

'Working professionally comes naturally to me. But I cannot work.'

'Things will change, give yourself a breather. I know it is easier said than done. You had a job and it was suddenly snatched away from you, and I can imagine how devastating it must have been for you, but don't let it break you and your professional aspirations. I will try my best to get you your work authorization back soon,' Mihir assured Neeti.

10

Enough of Running Around

Mihir could not bear to see Neeti losing weight and getting paler by the day. She was trying to be happy but deep down the loss of her work authorization was eating away her insides, so Mihir decided to apply for a green card under the EB-1 category right away. There are several categories under which people can apply for a green card, and people who are in the US on employment-based visas can apply for an employment-based green card. There are subcategories within this category, such as EB-1, EB-2, and EB-3, where EB stands for 'Employment-Based'. EB-3 is for professional, skilled, and other workers. It usually has a long waitlist due to the numerous applications filed under this category because many people fall under EB-3. EB-2 is for persons of exceptional ability and advanced degree professionals, and EB-1 is for persons of extraordinary ability. Considering his background, education, and experience, Mihir was an ideal candidate to apply under the EB-1 category. Not many people are eligible under this category and therefore if your application gets approved, you could get your green card as early as six months, depending on the number of applications received at the given time. Also, while applications under EB-3 and EB-2 are filed by the employer, an individual is allowed to file their green card under the EB-1 category.

Mihir started his EB-1 application. He began collating all the documents and getting together all the attestations required. He also needed recommendation letters from his employer, which they happily provided. He spent many months putting his application together, which involved writing a petition, providing the reasons why he deserved a green card, submitting letters of support from his colleagues and peers, and furnishing proof of the work that he had done so far which made him eligible to get a green card.

'You're working so hard on this. I wish I could be of more help,' Neeti said.

'You did help me with the petition. The rest of the work is more of coordination and getting the letters of support from everyone,' Mihir replied.

'Are we still waiting on some letters?'

'Yes, a couple of letters from my lab in Kansas City.'

'Okay.'

'Let's get out of Baltimore. You have been home for quite a few days and I have been working on my application. I think both of us need a getaway.'

'Sounds good.'

'There is a star watch party in Pennsylvania. I know how much you love the night sky. Let me check if there are any spots available.'

'That would be wonderful.'

Mihir checked on the website and luckily, there were a couple of spots still available. They prepared for the trip, got the essentials like mosquito repellent, emergency urine bags, and emergency lights. Red lights were the only kind of lights allowed as other lights could distract people from watching the stars. They left on Friday evening and drove to the venue. They had booked a cottage right in the middle of the mountains and Neeti loved it. Mihir was delighted to see a smile on Neeti's face.

They freshened up at the hotel and got ready to go to the venue. It was in the middle of a forest, a designated field from where you could camp and see the night sky clearly. The path to the venue was dark and scary and Mihir teased Neeti that they might encounter bears on the way. They reached the venue and it was pitch dark. They switched on their red lights and located the reception area. They were directed to the dining area which had a few lights on. They had sandwiches and coffee before heading towards the open field.

There were thousands of people with hundreds of tents in the field. Most people had opted to spend the night in tents rather than in hotel rooms, unlike Neeti and Mihir. It was chilly outside and Neeti was glad they had decided to stay at the hotel instead. But once she looked up, her heart skipped a beat. The whole sky was covered with a million twinkling stars, it looked as if someone had spilled a bottle of glitter in the sky. She could see the whole Milky Way. She was speechless; she had not seen anything like this in her life before. It was mesmerizing. She reached for Mihir's hand and held it tight. Mihir could feel Neeti's excitement and could not be happier. He put his arm around her and held her close. They spent almost the whole night gazing at the sky. Many people had brought telescopes and they let people use them. Neeti and Mihir went around the whole field and realized what an amazing planet they were living on. They finally retired to their hotel at around 4 a.m.

They woke up six hours later and spent the day amidst nature. They were finally breathing without worrying about visas or green cards.

'Life is beautiful; we only deprive ourselves of this beauty because of the things we choose to see,' Neeti said.

'We should have done this earlier.'

'I am glad we could do it now.'

'If I knew this would make you so happy, I would have done it last fall.'

'We all need to go through pain to realize how important it is to smile, I guess.'

'You didn't deserve that pain.'

'There are people who are going through worse.'

'That doesn't mean your pain doesn't exist.'

'But it does help me understand and appreciate the importance of what I have and how precious it is.'

'I am positive things will work out soon.'

'I hope so too, but even if they don't right now, eventually they will.'

'Promise me, you will never cry again thinking about your job situation.'

'I don't make promises I can't keep, but I will try my best.'

'I love you,' Mihir said, holding Neeti's hand.

'I love you too,' Neeti said, resting her head on Mihir's shoulder.

They returned home on Sunday night. Mihir had a workday on Monday, so they called it a night earlier than usual as they were both tired after the drive. Mihir was still working on his green card application, so his days were longer than usual. He would come back home from the lab and then spend a couple of hours every night working on his application. Gradually, the application was shaping up and he had started compiling all the documents together. After he received all the letters of support and put together all the attachments, it turned into a hefty folder.

'Phew! I didn't realize it would turn out to be this massive,' Mihir said.

'I am just amazed how hard you must have worked to put all this together.'

'It was a lot of work, but I didn't mind it at all. I can do anything to improve the quality of our life.'

'Thank you, Mihir.'

'You don't need to thank me. I am thankful to you for going through so much and finally coming out strong.'

'Okay, let's send this out.'

'Would you like to come with me to the post office?'

'Of course!'

Mihir applied for the green card under the premium processing category, which meant paying extra fee to get the results in fifteen days. Mihir and Neeti both were eagerly waiting for a response to the petition, and fifteen days later, they received a letter from the USCIS. It was a Request for Evidence, better known as RFE. What that meant was that USCIS needed more information and evidence to process their application. The massive folder that Mihir had provided was probably not enough and therefore he needed to provide additional information about his work and reasoning as to why he deserved a green card.

'It's not a rejection letter, at least. We still have our hopes alive,' Neeti said.

'I honestly thought my application was strong.'

'I thought so too, but we don't really know how these things work. I think this is the second chance we have got, and we cannot take it lightly, I think we should consult the specialists and respond to the RFE through an attorney.'

'I guess you are right.'

'One of my classmates was working with an immigration law firm. I believe that's one of the best immigration law firms in the country. I think we should consider hiring them.'

'Do you want to schedule an appointment during the day tomorrow? We will meet them in person for an initial consultation. I don't want to do the consultation over the phone.'

'Sure.'

Neeti contacted the law firm and scheduled an initial consultation. They went to the law office and a very friendly lawyer gave them a run-down of everything they should expect during this filing and all that was required to be done.

'We are doing this so that Neeti can get her work authorization as soon as possible,' Mihir said.

'We will try our best. We cannot guarantee you that the application will get accepted, but we can assure you that we will prepare the strongest application possible.'

Although the law office was to send the RFE back, Mihir had to do most of the work by reaching out to more people and also gathering more evidence proving his accomplishment as a researcher. After a month of hard work, he had finally put together all the documents required for the RFE. The lawyers added all the legalese and the required cases to cite, and Neeti and Mihir felt confident about their RFE. With hopes in their hearts and prayers on their lips, they sent out their response to the RFE. The decisions are usually sent out relatively quickly, so Neeti and Mihir were expecting a turnaround time of about fifteen days.

Nevertheless, they checked the mailbox for the letter every day. After fifteen days, they received a response from USCIS. Their application had been denied. The evidence that

Neeti and Mihir provided was not sufficient. Mihir was hugely disappointed but did not show it because he knew if he got weak at this point, it would break Neeti completely.

'You know what? We can apply for the green card again, there is no limit on how many times you can try. I just need to finish some of my experiments and write a couple more research papers, and then we will try again.'

'I really don't know if I should hope anymore.'

'Don't let this rejection dampen your spirits.'

'We tried and I can't thank you enough for spending all your energies for so many months just on one thing—how to make me happy. Our application got rejected. I am sad but I have you, and that's more important than anything else,' Neeti said as she reached for Mihir's hand. But she couldn't sleep that night. Mihir tried to comfort her, but it didn't work.

Neeti didn't sleep for the next couple of nights. She was trying not to get upset, but her body was defying all her commands. Mihir tried his best to comfort her, but Neeti was getting frail due to sleep deprivation. The rejection of the green card application had dashed Neeti's hopes to get work authorization, at least for now. Although she was tired of complaining about it, she thought about it constantly. One morning, Neeti got up from bed and made herself some black coffee and looked at her phone. She browsed through the contact list and saw Shekhar's phone number. The last correspondence she had had with him was when she had updated him about her graduation. She hadn't had her breakfast and was in no mood to eat. It was almost 7 p.m. in India and she wondered if it was too late to call Shekhar. She decided to text him instead.

'Hi, Shekhar. How have you been?'

'Hi, Neeti. I'm doing well. How have you been?' Shekhar responded immediately.

'I am back to square one, Shekhar. Navigating the system was painstakingly difficult and when I thought I had managed to overcome all the hurdles, life threw another curveball. I am back on a dependent visa and I don't know when I will get work authorization again.'

'Oh, I thought you were over that stage. When did this happen?'

'Recently. Now I have to keep waiting in the wings even after getting a law degree until I get my work authorization.'

'Do you know when that will happen?'

'No, there is no certainty about that. I know that it will happen eventually, but when? I don't know.'

'Tell me how can I help?'

'Suggest me something that I can do.'

'Are you open to coming back to India for some time, until you are sure of getting work authorization there?'

'I didn't consider that option, and I am not entirely sure if I am open to leaving Mihir here and going to India until the job situation works out here.'

'All right, think about it. I will email you the contact details of one of my friends, Ambar Saxena. He is a lawyer and was looking for someone well versed with US laws to join his team. If you think coming back to India is an option you would like to explore, send him your resume. I will give him a heads up just in case you decide to contact him.'

'Thanks, Shekhar.'

Neeti kept thinking about Shekhar's suggestion but did not want to leave Mihir all alone in the US and go to India. It felt outright selfish to her. They had been in a long-distance relationship for a long time before tying the knot and she knew how difficult it was for them to sustain the relationship. She did not want to be in that situation again. But she also didn't want her to be here half-heartedly when she knew she could work in India.

She decided not to leave the US.

Neeti could not volunteer with the law group that she did her externship with because she did not have her work authorization, which prohibited her from accessing patient records. Nonetheless, she wanted to try and explore other avenues where she could utilize her legal education and experience. She wanted to start volunteering again but the dates of her bar exam were quite close, so she decided to completely focus on the latter for now. The exam preparation would take up the next three months, so she called everyone to let them know that she would not be available for that period. She updated her WhatsApp status to 'Do not disturb' and deactivated all her social media accounts.

'Hi, Papa. How are you doing?' she called and asked her dad, Aseem.

'We are doing well. How are you and Mihir doing?'

'We too are doing well. Just wanted to let you know that I won't be available for the next three months.'

'Why? What happened? Is everything all right with you and Mihir?'

'Yes, everything is okay. I am preparing for my bar exam. It needs complete focus and I probably will not even get out of my room. I have joined a bar preparation course, so I will have daily reading and writing assignments, lectures, and tests.'

'You have to take another exam? We thought you were done with studying!'

'I had almost decided on not taking the exam because I don't have work authorization currently. But then I thought that once I become an attorney, it would probably be easier for me to at least volunteer with a law group. To become an attorney, I need to pass this exam.'

'We trust you but you really need to learn to take breaks and take it easy in life. Ever since you have moved to the US, you have been working hard on some goal or the other.'

'I know, I also want to relax. I will take a break once I become an attorney. For now, I need to give my 100 per cent to this preparation. The bar exam is supposedly one of the most difficult exams in the life of a law student, and I need to prepare myself mentally before I can start reading the prep materials.'

'Good luck and take care of your health. Soak some almonds overnight and have them the next morning.'

'Do tell her to peel the almonds before eating them,' Aanandi told Aseem as she stood close by.

'Yeah, Maa, I know that. You take care of yourselves and I will talk to you after my exam.'

Neeti had decided to take the bar exam but she did not know what she had got herself into. The preparation schedule was unforgiving and she did not even have time to eat, let alone cook anything. Mihir took care of cooking, cleaning, groceries, laundry, and everything related to the household. Neeti locked herself in a room, and at times Mihir would feed her as Neeti would finish her reading assignment. She would get exam-related nightmares almost every night, and Mihir would gently hug her and help her get back to sleep.

'Neeti, you are running a fever. You look in a pretty bad shape. You need to take a break,' Mihir continued.

'If I take a break, I will fall behind the schedule.'

'This isn't the time to think about your study schedule. You need to be in bed.'

Mihir carried Neeti in his arms and gently placed her on to the bed and fed her a peanut butter sandwich before giving her an over-the-counter tablet for fever. She immediately fell asleep. The next morning, she was still running a temperature and Mihir took the day off. He made ginger tea for Neeti and gave her another tablet in a bid to counter her fever.

'You need to learn to take breaks. You are killing yourself,' Mihir said feeling concerned about Neeti's condition.

'Just one more month and I would be on the other side of this ordeal,' Neeti replied bravely.

She continued with the rigorous study schedule for another month, and he took care of the household and her. She took the test and was finally relieved.

'I don't care if I fail or pass, I know this was the best I could have done.'

'I'm glad we are done with your exam. What lawyers are made of to survive such brutality is beyond me,' Mihir replied.

'No matter what the result is, I will always remain thankful for your help and support. I would not have been able to take this exam but for all that you did for the household and me.'

'Your goals are my goals, just like mine are yours!'

The results were two months away and Neeti and Mihir decided to take a break from the routine. They went on a little vacation and came back refreshed and rejuvenated. Neeti was so exhausted by the preparation that all she wanted now was to be home and do nothing. For the first time she was thankful that she could be home without having to wake up to alarms. She met up with some of her Indian community friends after a long time. Pragya introduced Neeti to some more women in the community and Neeti spent her days talking to them, socializing, and learning new skills from them. She learned to make Rajasthani cuisine from Aastha Kothari, one of the women Pragya introduced in the group. She realized how much effort it took to prepare those delicacies.

'You cook really well, and I don't mean to say it in a demeaning way,' Neeti told Aastha.

'I didn't get that. It's a compliment. Why do you think I would consider it demeaning?'

'For some reason, especially after coming to this country, I have seen many people treat housewives as women who are only good at cooking and doing household chores. They compliment you in a way that it almost feels like they are making fun of you and your lowly existence. I genuinely meant that you cook well.'

'Thanks, I really thought you were genuinely complimenting me. A lot of people compliment me for my cooking skills. If I thought like you, I would have felt miserable and would have died out of embarrassment by now. What they mean is up to them, what I make of those compliments is what really matters to me. I cannot let them decide my worth.'

'Thanks, Aastha.'

'Why? What happened?'

'Nothing. Do you like being a housewife?'

'I never thought about it, to be honest. I just do what I love doing and I'm happy living the life that I'm living. I have my hands full. Someone or the other is always over my place to learn cooking and on weekends, I cook for the homeless kids. So, I've never really had the time to think about it, but now that you've asked, I think I like it. Why do you ask?'

'Wow, that's really nice! This is the first time I have met someone here who is happy being a housewife.'

'It's all a matter of perception. Back home I was a teacher and loved my job. Here I teach cooking to women around and that makes me happy. I am still teaching. What I do is pretty satisfying and it keeps me busy during the week and even on the weekends. I know on my visa I cannot get paid, but this is something I can do which helps me feel that I am doing something good for the community and I sleep peacefully at the end of the day. If you want to call me a housewife, I don't take offence, but honestly, I don't understand why we need all these brackets to define people on what they are doing with their lives.'

'Makes perfect sense. Can I help you? I can come over to your place every weekend and I can help you cook and pack the boxes.'

'Sure, why not, the more the merrier.'

Neeti made *gatte ki sabzi* that she had learned from Aastha and flaunted it before Mihir. Mihir could tell Neeti was finally enjoying her break after the backbreaking preparation for her bar exam.

'You seem to be in a great mood,' Mihir said as he dipped the *chapatti* in the gravy.

'Focus on the food, I learned it from Aastha. Pragya introduced her to me. She cooks really well and she also prepares and distributes food to homeless kids on the weekends. I'm going to be helping her from this weekend onwards.'

'That sounds really good. What matters the most to me is that this is making you happy.'

For the next few days, Neeti kept reflecting on what Aastha had said about being a housewife. 'She looks so content, I think it's all a matter of perception. I was getting affected by all those random comments from people because I was letting them decide my worth, despite knowing about all the achievements I had till date with my hard work and dedication and why I chose to come over here and be a housewife. It was my mind that was playing games with me, others were merely props,' she thought.

Neeti started helping Aastha during the weekends and Pragya would also drop by on some weekends. They would have a nice time together and it gave a sense of belonging and satisfaction to Neeti.

It was time for Neeti's bar exam results. She didn't have the heart to check the results which were to be released on the Board of Law Examiners' website and were available to the general public, and you could view the list of the students by their roll numbers and could see if they failed or passed. Neeti asked Mihir to check the results for her. She couldn't sleep the night before. The next day Mihir went to the lab and Neeti was in a state of hysteria. The results were supposed to be out at 4.30 p.m. She gave strict instructions to Mihir that he should call or message only if she had passed. If she didn't get any call or message from Mihir after the results were out, she would understand that she had failed.

Neeti tried distracting herself by watching some random show on TV, but her eyes were fixated on the clock. She hardly ate anything. She wanted to throw up and wished that she'd pass out instead of dealing with this anxiety.

It was 4.30 p.m. and Neeti's hands started sweating. She looked at her phone—there was no call, no message. She kept looking at the clock and her phone alternatively and it was now 4.35. Her hopes were turning into disappointment. She knew Mihir would never keep her waiting like this if she had passed. 'It doesn't take more than a couple of minutes to check the results unless the website is down,' she thought. She went online and checked; the website was not down.

It was now 4.45. She went to the kitchen to get some water. She was heartbroken. The moment she entered the kitchen, her phone started ringing. By the time she came back to the living room, it had stopped ringing. There were two texts and a missed call.

'Congratulations!!!' the text read.

'My meeting ran over and I knew you would be anxious. I ran out as soon as the meeting got over and checked the results,' the other text read.

Neeti called Mihir back and started crying as soon as she heard his voice.

'You are an attorney!' Mihir said excitedly.

Later that evening when Mihir came back home, Neeti hugged him tight and thanked him for all his help and support during the bar preparation.

'I couldn't have done this without your support.'

'You are my support system. How could I not support you when it came to aiming for your goals?'

They celebrated her results with some ice cream and carrot cake. Neeti called her parents and friends and everyone congratulated her. Everyone wanted to know which area of law she would now practice, which brought her back to the same question – even after working and studying so hard why she still could not work.

Mihir looked at Neeti and it was clear from her face that she wasn't happy about her current situation. She was trying to make peace with her life by attempting to find joy in socializing with the people around, volunteering, and doing household work, but she definitely deserved more. But before that, she probably needed a good break.

'Why don't you visit India for a few days? That will give you the much-needed and well-deserved break. You haven't met your parents in a long time. I think this is the perfect time to go and meet them.'

'This actually sounds good. Maybe this is exactly what I need to do right now. Mihir, I didn't want to consider this option, but since I am going to India now, I just wanted to think about what Shekhar had suggested to me recently.'

'Oh, you spoke to Shekhar today?'

'No, I spoke to him a couple of months ago. He said one of his friends who is a lawyer is looking for someone well versed with US laws. I'm a fresh graduate and a new attorney so I'm not sure if that would fit the bill, but it wouldn't hurt to go and meet him or talk to him, at least.'

'You could have told me about this earlier. I would have definitely encouraged you to try it out.'

'It's in India.'

'I know that, but you are an attorney now. You need to utilize all this education and training. Trust your heart and do what's best for you.'

'I don't think I can stay away from you for long, but let me go and see.'

Neeti flew to India and did not book a return flight. She wanted to test the waters before taking the plunge, but wanted to at least give it a try.

11

India Calling

Neeti reached Indira Gandhi International Airport at 2.30 a.m. Although she was away for many years, the moment she landed, she felt as if she had never left the country. While it was dark outside, one could see sunshine on Neeti's face.

'Ma'am, do you need any help with your luggage?' the ground staff politely asked.

'No, I'm good. Thank you,' Neeti replied with a smile.

Her ride to the hotel was ready.

'Ma'am, I will take care of the luggage, you please go and sit inside,' the driver said, as he moved the bags from the cart to the car trunk.

'Thank you, *bhaiya*,' Neeti replied warmly.

She checked into a hotel in Aerocity for the night. The warm and friendly hotel staff made Neeti feel at home, although she was still not home yet.

'Reached?' Mihir texted.

'Yeah, I'm actually in the hotel room now, but dead tired. I'll do a video call before boarding my flight to Dehradun tomorrow,' Neeti wrote back.

She got up the next morning, did a quick video chat with Mihir, and got a ride to the airport that the hotel had arranged for her. As she boarded the flight, her heart started racing. She was excited to see her parents after being away for so long, the last trip she had made was three years ago which she had to cut short because of an urgent work issue.

Neeti's parents were already waiting for her at the airport when she reached Dehradun. She hugged them and they drove back home. Aanandi took Neeti's hand in hers and held it until they reached home.

'Do you want to freshen up? I have made *gajar ka halwa* for you. I will quickly make tea for everyone,' Aanandi said.

'Let me come and help you,' Neeti said placing her handbag on the dining table.

'What is there to help in making tea? Halwa is already prepared. You can help me in the kitchen once you get over the jetlag.'

'When is the return flight?' Aseem asked.

'I haven't booked the return ticket yet. I might work from here for some time.'

'Have you got your work authorization?'

'No, that's the reason I want to explore the option of taking up a job here.'

'And what about Mihir? He will live alone there?'

'Papa, let me think about it. I said I want to explore this option.'

'Discuss all these things later, let's have tea first,' Aanandi said as she brought steaming cups of ginger tea and *gajar ka halwa* in a tray.

Aseem got up and took the tray from Aanandi's hands and placed it on the coffee table. They chit-chatted for a while and then Neeti went to her room to arrange her clothes in the cupboard.

'Do all this tomorrow. Come sit with me for some time,' Aanandi said.

Aanandi was sitting on the bed and Neeti placed her head on Aanandi's lap.

'Do you miss us? Because of health issues, it's difficult for me to travel such a long distance, else I would have loved to visit you every year,' Aanandi spoke her heart out.

'I know that, that's why I never pressed you and papa to come and visit me. I miss you both a lot,' Neeti said, taking Aanandi's hand in hers.

'I miss the time when you lived with us. You remember how much you loved helping me with cooking and with other chores? I used to ask you to study and you would insist on stirring the *masala* every time I made *rajma*.'

'I used to love being home Maa, I loved doing household chores, and now things have changed so much.'

'What has changed?'

'I don't know, something inside me. When I was living here with you and papa, I loved spending time at home. Even when I was working in Mumbai, I used to tell Vandana that she should never feel ashamed of doing household work. But when it came to me being a housewife, all hell broke loose and I just could not handle it.'

'Oh, I thought it was just that one time when we had a conversation about it long back. I had no idea you were thinking about all this even after that. You should have called and talked to me.'

'I probably should have, but then I got busy with work and school, but now that I am back to being a housewife, I am struggling with these thoughts again.'

'Don't worry, now that you are here, we will talk about it at length. For now, get some rest.'

The next morning, Neeti got up and made tea for everyone, she was feeling a sense of calm with Aanandi and Aseem around. Everyone who has left India to settle in a different country probably feels this way when they return to their home countries, to their parents and loved ones. The country you had grown up in remains close to your heart, no matter how far you move away and for how long.

Aseem then went out to water the plants and the lawn. This was a morning ritual for him, taking care of the house and the little creatures it nurtured. The rose plant had a new bud and he was delighted to see this new addition to his plant family. He called Aanandi and Neeti and flaunted the little red blossom with pride. While Aseem continued with the trimming and grooming of the plants, Aanandi and Neeti came back to the living room.

'Would you like to have *poha* for breakfast?' Aanandi asked Neeti.

'Let me make it. I learned to make really scrumptious *poha* from one of my friends recently.'

Once the breakfast was ready, Neeti called Aseem inside and they had *poha* together. Aseem headed to a friend's place to discuss the new health policy for the retirees, and Neeti and Aanandi went to the terrace.

'I have a couple of clothes to dry. I washed them this morning,' Aanandi said.

As soon as they reached the terrace, the doorbell rang. It was Aanandi's domestic help, Poonam.

'We are here at the terrace. You can go ahead and start working. We will come downstairs in a bit,' Aanandi yelled from the terrace.

'Okay, Aunty,' Poonam hollered in return.

Neeti and Aanandi hung the clothes on the clothesline and came back to the living room. Poonam had swept the floor by then and was now mopping it.

'Oh, I don't want to ruin the floor,' Neeti said, as she tried walking hesitantly.

'*Arey*, *didi*, you go ahead. I will do that side again,' Poonam said.

'No, no, I will remove my slippers and walk. I don't want you to do it all over again.'

'Aunty, what is *didi* talking about? Tell her it's not a big deal,' Poonam said with a smile.

'She's forgotten how much she used to trouble me when she was little and I used to do the chores. She is behaving all grown up now. You finish your work quickly. I have got a *kurta* for you. Try it on and show me,' Aanandi told Poonam.

Poonam liked the *kurta* and left Aanandi's home wearing it. After Poonam left, Neeti and Aanandi went to the kitchen to get the lunch ready.

'I am making your favourite *rajma*,' Aanandi said.

'I will stir the *masala*!' Neeti said excitedly.

'So, tell me, what has been bothering you?' Aanandi asked as she started peeling the onions.

'Have you ever felt that you could do much more than just being a housewife?'

'This question has a lot of layers, just like this onion. Things were different when I got married. Your dad had a transferable job and we moved around a lot, so it didn't feel like a feasible option for me to work at that time. Once you were born, I consciously decided to focus on you. Taking care of you was no less than a full-time job, and once you were all grown up, I had gotten so used to being at home that it never felt odd to be home. For me, I was working 24/7 and it never crossed my mind that I needed to work; I already was.'

'But you were educated. Did you not feel that you could utilize your education and contribute to society?'

'Why do you think I did not contribute to society? In our days, there was no social media, most of the social exchanges happened in-person. Wherever we would go, I would make sure to join socially engaging groups. I worked with women in the community to raise awareness about women's health issues. Even in the neighbourhood, we would discuss issues that concerned us and then come up with resolutions. That is at a large scale. To me, my biggest contribution to society has been meaningful discussions with your dad. He never took any decisions without consulting me. He still doesn't, and I do the same, and above everything else, I raised you right.'

'That makes sense.'

'You don't have to necessarily agree with me. Everyone has different parameters for satisfaction. You like working professionally, and there's absolutely nothing wrong with it. In fact, I am really proud of you for always being so proactive and taking your professional goals seriously. But what bothers me is that you are reducing your entire existence to your professional identity.'

'I guess you are right, but I need to internalize all this.'

'Exactly. Don't go by what others say, good or bad. At the end of the day, what really matters is what your heart says. You cannot defy yourself for long. If you truly believe you can have a fulfilling life irrespective of your professional status, only then will it work, otherwise it won't. Don't rush into it, give yourself some time.'

'Thanks, Maa. Let me stir the *masala* now.'

Neeti was home after a long time and tried to spend every second of her day with Aseem and Aanandi. She watched their favourite shows on TV and also indulged in some neighbourhood gossip. She enjoyed her stay and was finding joy in the little things in life. She did all this for a few weeks, but she did not want to entirely dismiss the possibility of working while she was there, and therefore thought of getting in touch with Ambar Saxena.

'I am thinking of giving Ambar Saxena a call,' Neeti told Aanandi.

'It doesn't hurt to talk to him and discuss the opportunity. You haven't booked the return ticket yet, so you have a lot of time to think through it.'

Neeti decided to text Ambar Saxena before giving him a call.

'Hi, Mr Saxena. My name is Neeti Varma and I got your contact information from Mr Shekhar. Is this a good time to talk? Let me know when I can call you on this number.'

'Hi, Neeti. Shekhar did talk to me about you. I will give you a call tomorrow. Currently, I am out of town and will be back in Mumbai tomorrow. Would 1 p.m. work for you? In the meantime, could you send me your resumé?' Ambar Saxena texted in a while.

'Sure, I will send it over right away. I look forward to talking to you tomorrow,' Neeti texted back promptly.

Neeti sent her updated resumé to Ambar Saxena and went over it so that she was ready for the conversation next day.

'Would you like to go to the mall this evening? Your dad is going out with his friends, so we can have our little girls' evening out,' Anandi asked Neeti.

'This sounds fun. Let's do it!' Neeti was excited.

Aanandi and Neeti took an auto-rickshaw to reach the mall which was a couple of kilometres away from their home. After shopping for some dresses and shoes, they went to the food court. Neeti was thrilled to see the *chaat* stalls and couldn't wait to try out all the snacks.

'Oh, I have missed all this so much for so long!' Neeti cried.

'I know how much you like all this. What would you like to have?'

'You grab a table to sit. I will go get the food.'

Aanandi placed all the shopping bags on a table and waited for Neeti to return. Neeti came back with a tray full of *tikki*, *papdi chaat*, *samosas*, and *gulab jamuns*. She also got some *chhole bhature* and *kulfi falooda*.

'Are you sure you can eat all this?' Aanandi asked rather surprised with the orders placed.

'You've no idea how much I have missed eating all this,' Neeti said gleefully.

'But you do have Indian restaurants there.'

'We do, but they don't make it this well. I wish Mihir and I had stayed back in Mumbai instead of moving to the US.'

'For the snacks?'

'No, generally. After the kind of struggle I have seen in the last few years, I feel that things would have been much different had we lived in Mumbai.'

'I'm sure Mihir doesn't feel the same way.'

'He doesn't, and that's why I'm not forcing him to return to India. He has professional aspirations and just because he married me doesn't mean he would have to give them up. But I miss the kind of independence I had vis-à-vis my work life.'

'You made a choice, Neeti. You were doing really well professionally and you know the kind of void you were feeling without a life partner. I get it that nobody should be presented with a situation in life where you have to choose either love or your career, the same reason why you don't want to force

Mihir to come back to India. But in your case, it happened, and you made a choice. You not only chose love but you also worked hard to get your career back on track. You secured your work visa, which wasn't a piece of cake. You got into a prestigious law school and passed the bar in first attempt. You are an attorney now! Give yourself some credit for what you have managed to do so far. It's just a little bump you are facing right now, don't let this demoralize you.'

'I guess you are right. I probably won't get this kind of time once I get my work authorization again. All I need to do is to make peace with being a housewife.'

'I think the initial few negative reactions and comments you got after moving to the US created this fear inside you that people would judge you for being a housewife. There would always be people who would judge you, whether you are a housewife or CEO of a company. The problem lies with them, not with you.'

'Thanks, Maa.'

Aanandi and Neeti returned home and Aseem was also back by then. Aseem and Aanandi called it a night and Neeti then called Mihir.

'Hey, you have almost forgotten about me,' Mihir said.

'Come on, you very well know that I think about you every day. But I would not deny that I am having the time of my life here. Mom and I went to the mall and had Indian snacks today. Feels like my soul is now satiated,' Neeti beamed.

'I know how much you like Indian snacks, and I am glad you are getting to spend some time with your parents. It was due for a long time.'

'How are you doing? How is everything back there?'

'Everything is okay. The weather is changing a little bit, quite a few people in the lab are feeling under the weather. I hope I don't get the bug from someone.'

'Have you got your flu shot?'

'I have, but the influenza virus mutates every year, so I'm not sure if that would help. Most people in the lab got the flu shot. They got the flu despite that.'

'Okay, take care of yourself. I am going to speak to Ambar Saxena tomorrow, you remember the guy whom Shekhar had talked to about any possible job opportunities.'

'Yeah, I do remember that. Good luck with your conversation. I will call you again tomorrow. Let me know how it goes.'

'Okay, I'm going to bed now. You have a nice day and I will speak to you tomorrow.'

The next day Neeti woke up and got ready for her call with Ambar Saxena. Although it was only a phone call, she got ready with all her documents, in case she needed to refer to them.

'It's not an interview, relax,' Aanandi told Neeti.

'I know, but I would rather be over-prepared than under-prepared.'

'You'll never change.'

Ambar Saxena dropped a text before calling and after a few minutes, he called Neeti on her home phone.

'Hi, Ambar this side, can I speak to Neeti?' Ambar said as the call got picked up.

'Hi, Mr Saxena. This is Neeti.'

'You can call me Ambar.'

'Oh, sure, Ambar.'

'So, I looked at your resumé. I see that you are a recent law graduate and were sworn-in as attorney recently. But you do have some experience working on contracts. We need someone who can draft contracts in compliance with US laws.'

'Yes, I have experience working on contracts and it happens to be one area of law that interests me the most.'

'That's good to know because some find it rather lacklustre. So, are you looking for a permanent position? Because we definitely need someone who can work with us permanently on US-based contracts. If not, we do hire consultants as independent contractors. So, if you want an assignment that is on a contractual basis, we can work out something for you. We usually do three-month contracts for the kind of assignments we have. As and when we get these contracts, we will get in touch with you to see if you are available to work on them.'

'Thanks, Ambar. Would it be a remote position or do I need to be in Mumbai?'

'For the permanent position, you would have to be in Mumbai. I will also have to consult with my partners and we will have you over for a formal interview for the position. For the contractual position, you can work remotely, provided you are available for Zoom meetings and video conferences.'

'Is it okay if I thought about it and got back to you in a couple of days?'

'Certainly. Take your time and keep me posted.'

'Thanks, Ambar. I appreciate your time and consideration.'

'Sure, you have a nice day ahead. Bye.'

After the conversation with Ambar, Neeti kept sitting on the couch for about ten minutes, holding the phone in her hand. She was not sure what the best option for her was at this time. Moving to Mumbai was a big commitment and would also mean starting from scratch. She would have to look for a place to live, set up the house, and start all over. Opting for the remote option sounded better – she could continue living in Dehradun with her parents and because it was for a three-month period to begin with, she would get to know if this was what she wanted to do. Based on how she felt, maybe she could commit for a longer term later.

'How did the conversation go?' Aanandi asked.

'It went well,' Neeti replied.

Aseem also joined the two and Neeti explained the two options to them. Everyone thought that the remote option was the better one at this time. Neeti called Mihir and told him that she probably would take up the offer to work remotely for a three-month period and would then decide the long-term plan once she had tested the waters. Mihir agreed that it was the better option of the two.

Neeti called and told Ambar that for the time being she would be interested in the remote position. Ambar started the paperwork to hire Neeti as an independent contractor/ consultant, and Neeti got her first assignment in a couple of days after all the formalities were completed. The whole process took about a fortnight.

Now that she was working full time, she moved into the room upstairs. It had an attached bathroom. Neeti converted the room into her makeshift office and started working on the contract she had received from Ambar.

'Neeti, come down to have food. You need to take lunch breaks at least,' Aanandi shouted.

'Coming, Maa,' Neeti replied. Neeti, Aanandi, and Aseem then sat down for lunch together.

'How do you like your new work assignment?' Aseem asked.

'I've just started researching the legal issues and I will start drafting the contract in a couple of days. Ambar has provided me a template to work on, but I am going to modify it. It looks too boilerplate.'

Neeti worked diligently on the contract and finished working on it in a couple of weeks and had video conferences with the client during that time to make sure they were satisfied with the terms and conditions. One day after finishing her work, she came down and realized that she had not had evening tea with her parents for more than two weeks. She checked her phone and she had received two missed calls and five texts from Mihir. The last she had spoken to him was two days ago. She read the messages and got to know that he was down with the flu. She immediately called him.

'Hey, I'm sorry. I just checked your texts and missed calls. How are you feeling now?'

'I'm okay now. Just had some temperature and body ache. I will be all right in a day or two. How have you been?'

'I was busy with some crucial negotiations with the client. Your throat sounds awful. I feel so bad about having missed your calls and messages. I just didn't look at my phone at all in the last two days.'

'Don't feel bad, it's just the flu. I should probably get some rest now. I will call you tomorrow.'

'Yes, please get some rest.'

'What happened?' Aanandi asked.

'Mihir is down with the flu.'

'Oh, is it bad?'

'He sounded a little weak, but he said he would be fine in a couple of days. I hope he has something in the freezer to eat. I wanted to ask him but he wanted to sleep and I didn't want to hold him up.'

'I hope he feels better soon. We have finished having our tea. Shall I heat up yours?'

'No, it's okay. I don't feel like having it. Let me go in and rest for a little while. I was sitting in the chair the whole day, so I'm feeling a little tired now.'

Neeti was missing Mihir and felt guilty that she was away from him when he was sick. Although she knew it was not something to get extremely worried about, she felt that had she been with Mihir, she could have taken care of him. She was hardly spending time with her parents also now and that thought coupled with Mihir's health made her upset.

The next morning Mihir gave Neeti a call and told her that he was feeling better. He also assured her that there was enough frozen food at home and she should not worry about him and enjoy her time with her parents and focus on her work.

'I should have been with Mihir,' Neeti told Aanandi.

'Don't be too hard on yourself. He can take care of himself. Mihir is a mature guy, he understands your situation.'

'But I've not spent time even with you and papa for many days.'

'Neeti, you don't get everything in life. Life always throws options at you and you have got to choose. If you want to work on these contracts, you can't be with Mihir and you will have to cut down on the time you spend with us. Once you settle down with your routine, you will be able to spend time with us like how one does on their usual workdays. You can spend time with us on the weekends. But yes, you cannot be with Mihir if you want to work, so that's the choice you need to make.'

'I understand that. I was just feeling bad that I spend my weekdays upstairs.'

'You are overthinking. We understand work commitments, we can't expect you to be spending time with us when you are busy working on your contracts. I did feel bad when you didn't have food on time, but that doesn't mean we are against you spending all your weekdays working diligently on your assignments.'

'Now that it's a weekend, I will spend every single second with you and papa.'

'Okay, listen. Do you remember your dad's friend Suhas uncle and his wife Sudha aunty?'

'Of course. How are they doing?'

'They are doing well. Their daughter Priya is getting married soon. Since we are so close to the family, we would be attending all the functions and ceremonies, and we need to help with the wedding preparations as well. Since you are here with us, would you like to come along?'

'What! That little Priya is getting married?'

'She isn't little anymore. She has been working in Delhi for the last five years or so and is now getting married to a guy she met through a matrimonial website. You should go and meet her.'

'I would absolutely love to meet her. Do you know who the guy is and what does he do?'

'I'm not able to recall his name. He lives in the US. I think he works in an IT company. Ask her when you meet.'

'When is the wedding?'

'A couple of weeks from now.'

That evening after finishing work, Neeti got ready to meet Priya. Aseem and Aanandi were already there, helping Suhas and Sudha. Their home was in the lane next to Neeti's, so she walked and reached in ten minutes. Everyone was excited to see Neeti. She paid regards to everyone and asked Sudha where Priya was and then went to the room where Priya was trying to select what to wear out of the two shortlisted dresses for her *haldi* ceremony.

'Hi, Priya,' Neeti said as she entered the room.

'Neeti *didi*! So good to see you. How have you been?'

'You remember me? It's been a long time.'

'Of course, I do. I used to come to you whenever I had any problems and doubts in understanding macroeconomics. I'm so glad you are in India currently and will be able to attend my wedding.'

'Have you decided which dress you would wear?'

'I have shortlisted two. I think I will go with the yellow one. Also, I am so tired now. I just want to sit and relax for some time.'

'Okay, I will leave then.'

'No, *didi*, stay. I wanted to talk to you about life in the US. I have done some research online and have also talked to some of my friends who live there but I still have this fear of the unknown.'

'Don't have any fears. You are a confident young woman; you will do just fine. What does your fiancé do? Do you know what visa you would be on?'

'Kapil is working with an IT company in California. He is on his H-1B visa currently, but his company would be filing his green card application soon.'

'That's good to know. Because as a dependent of someone on an H-1B visa, you would not be able to work until Kapil's green card application is accepted.'

'I think I am okay with that for some time. I want to spend some time with Kapil, especially since we met online and haven't spent much time together.'

'I'm glad you are open to not working for some time, but it does get lonely without a professional life there, so make sure you have something constructive to do while you are on your H-4 visa.'

'I have been working for a while now and only after I started my matrimonial search did I realize that I don't connect with most people. I finally found Kapil with whom I can be myself without any inhibitions, so I am ready to put my professional life on hold for a few years and build a strong relationship with him. It's never an easy decision to choose between love and career, but I don't think I can find anyone like Kapil again, and I am going to try and get my H-1B visa if his green card application gets delayed for any reason. I also have some friends in California and Kapil has a group of friends too, so I think I would be fine.'

'I am positive you would do fine, but do a thorough research about life in the US before moving there. I wish I had met you earlier, but there is still some time to prepare yourself mentally. Things are very different in the US, the neighbourhoods aren't like how we have here, and most people keep to themselves. But since you already have some friends there, that would make your life easier. Not having a work life can be an issue because there is not much to do at home, so unless you have a plan to volunteer, you would have to figure all this out after moving there, which could be a challenge. If you have any time on your hands amid all the wedding preparations, do try to find out what kind of volunteering opportunities are available there.'

'Thank you, *didi*. This is very helpful. I'm so glad you came here and we could talk about all this. Everyone paints a rosy picture about moving to the US. I had no idea about the things that you just told me about.'

'I learned things the hard way and had to figure things out on my own, so I am more than happy to help. If you have any questions, don't hesitate to give me a call.'

Neeti, Aanandi, and Aseem walked back home together. Neeti called Mihir after she reached home. He was recovering well and Neeti finally felt better. She spent that entire weekend with her parents and did not even open her laptop to check her emails.

On Monday morning she received a text from Ambar.

'Hi, Neeti. The client is really happy with the guidance and assistance you provided them. My partners and I were wondering if you would be interested in considering the permanent position in our office.'

Neeti looked at the text and did not respond immediately. She checked her email and she had got an offer to work on another contract in the meantime. She closed her laptop and went downstairs. Aanandi was sitting on the couch and Neeti placed her head on Aanandi's lap.

'Are you all right?' Aanandi asked.

'I have been away from home for three months. I miss home. I miss Mihir.'

'You know that you can go back any time. Don't you?'

'I do. But I have got an offer to work on another contract, it's sitting in my inbox. I also got an offer from Ambar to consider the permanent position. They seem to be impressed with my work.'

'And here you are lying on the couch with your head on my lap.'

'Why does life have to be this sadistic?'

'It's not sadistic; the more you want to complicate it, the more entangled it becomes. You can always choose simplicity. Looks like your dad is back. He had gone to Suhas uncle's place to help with the wedding arrangements.'

'Priya was singing your praises, Neeti. What did you guys talk about?'

'I just talked to her about life in the US and how she needs to be aware of it and work around the challenges in general over there.'

'She sent chocolates for you and said thanks.'

'She is sweet.'

'She wanted me to ask you to stay in touch with her once she moves to the US.'

'Sure, but she is moving to California, it's the other end of the country. We live on the East Coast. But I will try to stay in touch. I didn't know she liked the conversation that we had so much.'

'You can contribute towards society and improve the lives of people without being a part of the workforce. This is exactly what I was trying to explain to you when you asked me how I was satisfied being a housewife despite being qualified and educated. You can always use your education, qualification, and experience to make a difference in the world, irrespective of your employment status. Just the way you did when you talked to Priya, without even realizing it,' Aanandi said.

'I guess that's true. I don't know how much of a difference I have made in anyone's life working on that contract for the last three months. I have spent most of my time upstairs, locked in my room. I hardly spent time with you both. I am away from Mihir, I didn't even get to know that he got the flu. He managed everything on his own even though he has been sick. And just by talking to someone, I made a difference to her perspective about something.

I'm not sure if I want to take up this new contract to work on, and I am going to say no to Ambar for the permanent position. It might take a few months or years for our green card application to get accepted, but until then, there is so much I can do with my life.'

'I'm glad you are thinking along these lines. You may be hungry for success, but that hunger shouldn't eat you away,' Aseem said.

'You can blog about your experiences in the US and help women get familiar with the new life. You can write about it. You can do so much with your time, and that would, in turn, help so many people,' Aanandi added.

'You should have seen the way Priya was talking about you. She was praising your clarity of thought and said she has so much to learn from you. You need to trust yourself a little more and get over your insecurities about being a housewife. Nobody cares for your employment status; they only care about how you make them feel. I understand some of your experiences have shaped your thought process but try and analyze all those incidents and you would realize that the comments were either from some people who were merely doing their jobs and checking the list of questions, or were from people who were neither related to you nor knew anything about you. Those innocuous questions or queer comments should not affect you or your self-esteem. You can do better,' Aseem remarked.

'Thank you, both of you. I'm glad I made this trip. I'm now ready for my trip back home.'

'Leave after attending Priya's wedding.'

'Of course! I cannot leave a chance to gorge on those yummy Indian snacks!'

And they all burst out laughing.

Neeti declined the offer for the new contract and politely refused to take up the permanent position that Ambar had offered. She attended Priya's wedding and Priya was delighted to see Neeti at the wedding. Priya was beaming as she was getting married to the man of her dreams and also because she was prepared to take over her new life in the US, armed with all the information that she had received from Neeti and the online searches.

Neeti booked her return ticket the next day and started packing her bags. She realized that she had totally forgotten to call Rhea during these three months. She picked up the phone and called her immediately.

'Hey,' Rhea said as she picked up the phone.

'Hey, I'm sorry I was in India for the last three months and I'm calling you a week before I'm about to fly back to the US.'

'Now that you have already apologized, I can't even get mad at you. Is there a possibility you can come over during this last week you are here?'

'No, I need to pack my bags and make sure I visit all the relatives before leaving, so that won't leave me with any time to travel. And what's the point of coming all the way to Kolkata if I cannot even spend a week with you there? The next time I'm in India, I'm going to visit you for a week.'

'You know that those "next times" never come.'

'Come on, Rhea. We are not those kinds of friends.'

'I guess you are right. Now tell me, how are you feeling now? I know your visa situation was troubling you a lot, and I wish we had talked about it at length while you were here in the same time zone. Otherwise, it's so difficult to match the timings.'

'There's no need for that anymore. This India trip has removed all my insecurities around being a housewife. I'm at peace and ready to deal with the circumstances head-on.'

'This is really heartening to know. But it isn't easy to accept that you are not allowed to work when you are willing and able because there are rules in place that prohibit you from working.'

'I completely agree with you. Not being able to work after having worked for years can be devastating. It can affect your physical and mental health. But every country has its immigration policies and rules in place. I probably should have read the rules about employment and work visas in detail before moving to the US, but even if I had read the rules, I would not have changed my mind about getting married to Mihir. Marriage is a beautiful thing and getting married to the person whom you love and connect with is the most important factor that guides that decision. Where the person lives is secondary. It just took me a long time to find that place where I am at peace with myself irrespective of my visa status. Finally, I have understood that the only way to deal with anything in life is to accept what you cannot change and take steps to improve the quality of life rather than indulge in self-loathing. Most importantly, your home is your castle. It should never feel like a prison, and I am so ready to go back to my castle.'

'I want to thank whosoever or whatsoever made you realize this aspect of life. I am so relieved to hear that you are finally at peace. From the time you moved to the US, you have been running around a lot. It almost felt that you were on a treadmill this whole time.'

'Yes, and finally I am out of that mental gym,' Neeti said with a big smile on her face.

'Next time you are here, let me know the day you reach. Keep in regular touch now and have a safe flight home.'

'Thanks, Rhea. You take care and I will speak to you again soon.'

Aseem and Aanandi went to the airport to see Neeti off. They were proud of their daughter and also the fact that she was going home stronger than ever. They wished her a happy flight, and Mihir was eager to receive her at the Baltimore International Airport.

The moment Neeti saw Mihir she realized how much she had missed him in the last three months. Her mind wasn't clouded with doubts, fears, or apprehensions anymore. She knew she wanted to be with Mihir and she was ready to deal with whatever life threw at her.

Mihir welcomed Neeti with a hug and was delighted to see her.

'You've grown up so much,' Mihir teased Neeti and gave her a snug hug.

'I'm sorry for being away from you for so long, and I'm sorry it took me this long to figure out what I wanted but I'm glad I'm finally where my heart is. I missed you so much.' Neeti said as she hugged Mihir back.

Neeti and Mihir returned home and after resting for a couple of days, Neeti started a blog about the experiences as someone living on a dependent visa in the US. She continued to help Aastha with cooking meals for homeless kids on the weekend and made sure she remained in touch with her friends, and called Aanandi and Aseem every day.

12

Life—A Mixed Bag of Experiences!

It was a beautiful spring morning. Birds were chirping and so were the little kids playing outside. Neeti was at the Rotunda shopping complex. There was an array of water fountains near the seating area and, no matter what time of the day it was, kids excitedly got drawn towards the water fountains as their parents ran after them to make sure they didn't get wet and fall sick later on. It was not summer yet and the weather would get tricky every now and then.

It was time for Neeti to return home; Pragya was coming over. She did not want to keep her waiting in case she decided to arrive sooner than the scheduled time. She walked back home swiftly after picking up some snacks from the departmental store but it was difficult to walk fast while ignoring the carpet of tiny purple, yellow, and pink flowers on the sidewalks. She took her cellphone out from her handbag and clicked a few pictures, it almost felt impudent to walk past the flowers without appreciating their beauty.

She came back home and drew open the curtains in the living room. As soon as she opened the windows, the pleasant spring breeze gently blew her hair, and the bright sun kissed her face, giving her dark eyes a hazel glow. It was a huge living room, compared to most living rooms in Baltimore. The sunlight coming from the three large windows had brightened the entire room. She looked out of the window and noticed that her favourite tree had finally started to grow back its leaves. It was a tall tree that looked like eucalyptus. Neeti was not sure as to what kind of tree it was but she thought that it was a peculiar one, and she loved to watch it every fall and spring. 'It probably is different, and not strange,' Neeti mused. In fall, it didn't shed its leaves until after every other tree had shed its leaves. It took its own sweet time. In spring, it was always the last one to grow the leaves back. It almost appeared that it didn't care about what the rest of the world did, it did what it wanted to do.

'It's different, not wrong, and there is a difference between the two, a huge difference,' Neeti thought to herself as she continued to look at the tree. She felt a strange connect with this tree because she too had done things in life that were against the norm. She looked at the tree and smiled. The tree probably didn't even know that Neeti existed, and also that she had found a pal in it, but that didn't bother Neeti. She found happiness in looking at the tree and that's all that mattered.

It was half past twelve and Neeti decided to make herself a cup of tea. One coffee in the morning probably wasn't enough. Besides, she loved tea, made the typical Indian way. She liked her tea strong, with copious amounts of tea leaves, a little milk, and just a hint of sugar, boiled to perfection. Ginger was a must, no matter what weather it was. As she was done looking at her favourite tree, she poured the tea into her favourite cup that read 'Hello Gorgeous' and settled on the couch with the cup of piping hot ginger tea in her hands, she got reminded of Vandana and their chat sessions over tea. Then suddenly the cellphone's beep broke her reverie. It was Mihir.

'How is it going?'

'Going well, I'm having tea. What are you up to?'

'Just finished an experiment, going for a seminar now.'

'Okay.'

'What's the plan for the day?'

'Pragya is coming over.'

'Great, hope you have a nice time with your friend. See you later in the evening.'

'See you.'

Neeti had recently signed up to volunteer with a law group working in the field of immigration law. As she was waiting for Pragya to come over, she started reading the handbook that the group had sent to her. She took the last sip of her tea and bookmarked the page as she got up to go to the kitchen to put the cup away. As soon as she placed the cup in the kitchen sink, her cellphone started ringing. She came back to the living room and picked it up. It was Pragya, she was at the entrance of the apartment complex.

'Hey, I'm here,' Pragya announced.

'Wait, I will come downstairs and open the door for you,' Neeti responded.

Neeti lived on the second floor. She sprinted down the stairs and opened the main door to the apartment complex. Neeti and Pragya then walked up the marble staircase. Neeti's apartment was the first one on the left corridor. She opened the door and a whiff of a sweet fragrance welcomed Pragya.

'Your home always smells lovely,' Pragya said taking in the fragrance.

'Yeah, this is my favourite and I love using it. Would you like some tea? I just finished mine not very long ago, but I won't mind another cup.'

'No, I am good. I just had my breakfast. By the way, it's beautiful outside.'

'It is, I just opened the windows...'

'...and started looking at that strange tree?'

'It's not strange, it's different.'

'All right, all right. How have you been?'

'I have been great.'

'That's really nice to hear.'

'My trip to India really helped as it made things clear to me. I just needed some clarity of thought and when I was away and assessed everything from a distance, I realized how much it meant for me to be with Mihir. I had a work assignment and it felt like I was just a machine. I think having a job makes sense only if you have your loved ones around.'

'I couldn't agree more with what you just said, and on that note, I want to give you some good news.'

'I can't wait to hear it. I just want everyone to be happy. Tell me, quick!'

'My husband had applied for a green card recently, and his application has been accepted!'

'Oh my God! This calls for a BIG PARTY! You have been on a dependent spouse visa for years! You waited for this patiently for so many years. I can't express right now how happy I feel for you. Give me a hug!' Neeti said as she got up to hug Pragya.

'I can't put into words what I am feeling right now.'

'I can totally imagine.'

'I have applied for my Employment Authorization Document (EAD) and can't wait to start working again. It's been ages since I last worked. I'm nervous as much as I'm excited.'

'You've maintained your poise and calm for so long. You so deserve this.'

'I have had my bad days. Now that I am past that stage, I can talk about it without feeling too vulnerable. I have had severe meltdowns to the point that I wanted to return to India for good. I also went to therapy because I was getting depressed thinking about my visa situation, work authorization, green card, and everything related to it. It was sickening—the same discussions everywhere, and everyone just wanted to talk about all that and pity me. It was breaking me from inside and I decided to get intervention before it was too late.'

'Why did you not tell me about all this!?' Neeti was mad.

'All this happened around the same time you lost your work authorization. You were already going through so much. I did not have the heart to talk to you about any visa-related stuff.'

'It was about your mental health. You should have talked to me about it. But it's okay, I am relieved that you went for therapy, so many people are ashamed to acknowledge that they need help and brush it under the carpet, only to turn the problem into a monster they can't deal with later on.'

'I know, there are so many women in the Indian community that I know need help but they just don't feel comfortable talking about their woes. These visa issues have a very creepy way to mess you up.'

'I totally agree with you. I am glad I could confide in my parents and come out stronger after having a heartfelt discussion with them. At times the issues seem much larger and horrific in your imagination than they actually are, and all you need is to pour it all out in front of someone you trust.'

'Exactly. The therapy not only helped me from losing my mind but also saved my marriage. I was having incessant fights with my husband. It was difficult for me to explain to him what I was going through, especially when it was all piling up for many years. He just saw an irritable, grumpy woman who was ever ready to pick fights with him, which was not always the case. After therapy, things changed drastically and that's when my husband realized that I was not a grumpy woman. It was my depression that was eating me away little by little every single day.'

'But it's all a thing of past now. Now you are eligible to work and would be able to live your life the way you want to.'

'Yes, I'm feeling extremely thankful. Any news on your work authorization part yet?'

'No, but I am not letting it affect me. I know it's just a temporary phase and I need to make the most of what I have right now.'

'You've always been a fighter. You were among the very few that I have known who secured their H-1B visa even after coming to this country on a dependent spouse visa. I know all that hard work would pay off soon.'

'I hope so too, but for now I am looking forward to my volunteering opportunity. Should we go for a walk? You are not having tea anyway, and it's gorgeous outside. Let's go to the tulip garden in Roland Park and spend some time smelling ... well ... the tulips.'

Pragya smiled. They went to the tulip garden which was within walking distance from Neeti's apartment. The weather made the walk all the more pleasurable. They both got pictures clicked at the garden and made the most of this beautiful spring day. Pragya went back to her home from the garden and Neeti came back to hers. She prepared lunch and then finished reading the handbook.

Mihir was back in the evening and as soon as he entered the home, he yelled, 'Guess what?'

'I have no idea,' Neeti responded.

'I have cleared the first stage of the interview for the assistant professor position.'

'Oh my God! Today is the day to get good news. Pragya's green card application got approved and now this. Congratulations!'

'That's good to hear. You guys are close. I am sure you must be happy that she is relieved. I need to prepare my slides for the next phase though. It would be a video presentation and meetings with everyone in the department for a day and a half.'

'I'm excited and also relieved for her, she has been waiting patiently for it for years. She even had some mental health issues because of her visa situation and she never talked to me about those. I was so mad at her but she said she did not want to disturb me when I was dealing with my own issues regarding my work authorization. Anyway, I am just thankful all that is now behind her and she can look forward to a satisfying work life. Let me fix an early dinner and then you can start working on your slides.'

Mihir was busy preparing the slides for his next round of interviews, and Neeti started volunteering with the law group working with people dealing with immigration law issues. She continued helping Aastha on the weekends with the meal preparations for the homeless kids.

Mihir's presentation went well and the department chair told him that they would get back to him in three weeks' time as they were also considering some other candidates for the position.

Pragya got her EAD in the meantime and started applying for various positions. She asked Neeti to help her with her cover letters explaining the gap in the resume. Neeti told Pragya that she didn't need to bother too much about it as she was not eligible to work during this time, and helped her write a cover letter explaining her situation and what kept her away from the workforce for those many years. She also did some mock interviews with Pragya so that Pragya could get a little more comfortable when she would need to go for the real ones. Pragya finally got called for an interview and because Neeti had some free time, she accompanied Pragya to the office where she was scheduled to go for the interview.

'I'm really nervous, I have not done this in years,' Pragya said upon reaching the office.

'You absolutely rocked the mock interviews. You will kill it, just go for it,' Neeti pepped up Pragya, infusing confidence in her.

Pragya then went inside for the interview, while Neeti waited for her at the reception. The company was a finance consulting group and had placed some handouts for financial planning at the reception area. Neeti picked one up and started reading it. In between, she would peep if Pragya was done with the interview. After about thirty minutes, Pragya came out smiling.

'I got selected! They will send me the formal offer letter in the mail, but they confirmed my selection at the end of the interview,' Pragya said, trying hard to contain her excitement.

'Wow, that's incredible! Congratulations! And you were so nervous for no reason!' exclaimed Neeti.

'I don't believe this is happening. I don't know how to react.'

'Don't say anything. Let's go and celebrate.'

Neeti and Pragya went to Hampden and had lunch together. Pragya hardly ate anything, her heart was full, and so was her stomach—with happiness. Pragya hugged Neeti one more time before leaving as her eyes gleamed with tears of joy.

'I can't put into words how thankful I am to you for your help and support. You were the strongest force of motivation for me all these years,' said a beaming Pragya.

Neeti teared up a little and wished Pragya the best as she was about to embark on the second innings of her professional journey. Neeti called her mom on the way back home and told her about Pragya's interview.

'You were right, Maa. You don't need to work professionally to make a difference in people's lives. The kind of satisfaction I feel after seeing the happiness on Pragya's face, I haven't felt in years. All you need is the right intention and will to help and support others.'

'I'm glad you have realized it. This will make your life so much easier. We also feel a sense of relief seeing you at peace,' Aanandi replied.

Neeti came back home and saw fresh flowers in a vase on the coffee table. Mihir was already home.

'Guess what?' Mihir asked.

'You got the job!' Neeti replied.

'And?'

'And what?' Neeti said with a smile.

'They are filing my green card application. Now that I would be an assistant professor, the chances of it getting declined are bleak. So, that means you will get your work authorization back pretty soon.'

Neeti ran to hug Mihir. A month later, Mihir's new employer filed his green card application, which got approved and Neeti applied for her EAD soon after. She applied for attorney positions and received a job offer from one of the public interest law groups that she keenly desired to work with.

Acknowledgements

Writing this book has been one of the most rewarding experiences of my life. Although it is the fruit of my labour, this book would not have come into existence without the encouragement from, and support of these incredible people.

First and foremost, I thank my husband, Raj for being my biggest support system, for trusting my abilities even when my confidence in myself dwindled, and for being my greatest cheerleader.

I am eternally thankful to my mom, dad, and siblings – Sanjeev, Manjula, and Poornima for always believing in me. I am equally thankful to my mother-in-law and father-in-law for their constant support.

A big thank you to Sachin Garg, author and dear friend, who read the very first draft of my manuscript and provided honest, detailed, and invaluable feedback.

I am immensely grateful to Ajay Mago, Publisher, Om Books International, and Shantanu Ray Chaudhuri, Editor in Chief, Om Books International for placing their faith in a first-time author like me and giving me this tremendous opportunity. My heartfelt thanks to Sheela Roy, Editor, Om Books International, for her warmth, empathy, and support during the entire editing process. A special thanks to Sumeet Kaur for her valuable assistance with the editing of the book. I couldn't have asked for a better team to work with on my debut novel.

I want to thank all my friends and well-wishers, especially my Twitter and Instagram families, for their unceasing encouragement, kindness, and love. They have helped me in more ways than one by being there when I needed them, and by cheering me up on days when I couldn't cheer myself up.

Last but not the least, thank you to all those living on spouse-dependent visas who are fighting a silent battle every day as the world goes about its business. Your perseverance, patience, and determination inspire me tremendously.